GOOD GIRL

ALAN LEE

Good Girl

by Alan Lee

First Edition
Printed in USA

Cover by Sweet 'N Spicy

Sparkle Press

 Created with Vellum

For Megan
Better family than I deserve

AUTHOR'S NOTE

Anterograde amnesia is a real disorder. Other than leveraging artistic license to extend memory loss before the incident, I've done my best to be true to its complications.

A temporary peace was by these means produced; but it proved only a calm before a more violent storm.
-William Russell

1

January 2nd.

Ankles crossed on the desktop.

The devil may care, but not I—I get dirt on my workspace when I *please*.

Steely eyes fixed on the computer screen.

Emails? Answered.

Scotch? Sipped. Barely. Then replaced in the drawer.

First day back in the office since overthrowing villainous regimes in Italy. And since recovering for a month. Because toppling regimes hurt.

I missed forty days of work and the commiserating income, but I wasn't worried. For one thing, I was married now and my doting wife had money and no qualms about disbursement. Not the most talented nurse, perhaps, but certainly the most affectionate and lavish. And second, I won a tournament in Italy and had been promised part of the winnings. To the victor goes the spoils, they told me, even though I burned down their house.

I didn't know how soon to expect payment, however. Just in case, I wasn't spending any of it. But I was declining a larger percentage of requests for my services than was financially responsible.

Because I didn't want to serve warrants.

I didn't want to locate lost spouses.

I didn't want to hide out in a car with a camera.

I enjoyed these and other mundane tasks to an extent. But at the moment, scrolling through my inbox, much of it struck me as banal. I could handle banality in February. Why else have a February? But not on January 2nd, for heaven's sake. It was a new year. I required stimulation and challenge.

The stairs outside my office door groaned, wooden slats creaking with use. Ah hah! Stimulation. A man leaned into my open doorway. Couldn't see him from the waist down. Hard looking guy, hair cut close, his face all sharp angles. Jacket but no collar. With his left hand, he knocked on my doorframe.

I stood.

"How you doin," he said. "Looking for Mack August. Got a job I need help with. You him?"

I picked up the Kimber 1911 pistol from my desktop. Clicked the hammer back and aimed the barrel at him.

"Contract's off," I said.

He didn't flinch. His face didn't pale. But he did look… disappointed. "Contract's off?"

"Check the database. Contract's off."

I referenced a bounty placed on my head by Darren Robbins. A hundred grand. He'd canceled the contract last month, but some of these mercenaries set up their account to only be alerted if the contract gets fulfilled, not canceled. Or else they miss the alert. For a hundred grand, they'll swing by Roanoke every few days and look to see if a light's on in the office. As part of the underworld code, a hit at home is off limits. Cause they're sweethearts. With databases.

The guy made a sniffing noise. "How'd you know? Who I was, I mean."

"You have a neck tattoo. No one with a heart of gold has a neck tattoo. Plus your accent isn't from Roanoke. Plus guys like you don't hire guys like me. Plus you hid your gun hand."

"Son of a bitch." He mumbled, referring to himself. I hoped. He raised up and returned the pistol to a holster behind his back. A hitman—but not a good one. "Waited all this time, got'damn it. Contract belonged to Robbins, right? Why'd that bastard cancel?"

"I told him if he didn't, I would feed him to his cat."

"Oh."

"But here's the best part—I'm going to kill him anyway."

He grinned. Wasn't a good look. "Want me to do it?"

"Negative."

"Why not?"

"You suck at this."

"Hell I do." Stood up a little straighter. "I'm a pro, guy."

"You just put your gun away." I waggled the Kimber. "While mine is still out and pointed at you. Kinda forecloses the *pro* argument. What if I was lying about the contract?"

Now his faced paled a little. "Shit."

"Uh huh."

"Were you? Lying?"

"I was not. But that doesn't change facts. Which are, you suck at this."

"Whatever, guy. I'm going," he said.

"Tell your friends. Contract's off."

"My friends?"

"You're the second today to show up. It's not even lunch. You idiots need to do your homework."

The guy made a sniffing noise again. Glared some. Left. The stairs groaning under his descent.

Darren Robbins. I was going to shoot him. A lot. Starting with his pinky toe. I set the gun on the desktop, feeling punchy. That was the wrong kind of stimulation.

Called for another shot of Johnny Walker Blue, though.

Thirty minutes later, as my anger burned off, the door opened on the main level and the stairs heralded another visitor. I placed my hand on the Kimber. I might just shoot this one.

A woman entered.

Gun down. I do not shoot women. Because I am a hero.

Also, for the most part, they don't shoot me.

She looked sheepish—unsure if this was the right place and unsure if private investigators were real people and unsure how to begin. Maybe fifty, fifty-five. Strong, like she worked for a living. Twill jeans that weren't new, weren't old. Not tight but not baggy. A cotton v-neck sweatshirt worn under a brown cardigan. Modish leather boots, low heel. No rings or other jewelry. She had faint lines at her eyes and lips—no plastic surgery, no makeup. Her arms were crossed and she was a little hunched against the cold.

"Mr. August?"

I stood. "Yes."

Embarrassed smile. "Do you have a moment?"

"For you, I have the best moments. Please come in."

She did. Glancing around, arms still crossed. A defensive posture. Looked at my bookshelves. Admired my potpourri.

I assume.

She asked, "You are for hire? Did I say that right?"

"I am and you did."

"You do all...I mean, I guess, I should say, what kinds of things do you do?"

"Things other people would rather not."

"Oh."

I nodded impressively. "Think of me like a police officer. But one you can have personally."

"Okay. That's what I was... Okay good." Her mind was made."

"Indeed."

"I'm Rose Bridges." She didn't offer her hand so I didn't either. A gentleman only shakes if the woman offers. "I'm here on behalf of someone who would like to speak with you. Is that okay, Mr. August?"

I indicated my chair. I sat. She sat. I nodded encouragingly.

"He could probably come himself, but this way is easier," she said. "Ulysses Steinbeck. Do you know him?"

Holy moly. What a name. Liked him already.

"Should I?"

She said, "Probably not. He was in the news a few years ago, and used to be a respected man about town. I was only curious."

"What event warranted his appearance in the news?"

"A bad car crash. That's part of the reason it's easier if you go see him." She withdrew a single check from her cardigan pocket. Didn't know what to do with it then. Pushed some of her hair behind her ear. Red hair on the verge of gray. "We'll pay you for your time. Of course."

"What relationship do you have to Ulysses?"

"I...I'm his caretaker."

"Full-time?"

"Yes. I live with him."

"Is he paying me or are you?"

"It's his money."

"What for?"

"What for?" she repeated.

"I mean, why does he wish to speak with me?"

"Oh. Yes, sorry, Mr. August. He needs your help."

"Help with...?"

"Well..." She laid the check on my desk and pushed it across. It was blank except for the signature. Holy moly, I liked him even more. Rose wore no fingernail polish. "You see, Mr. August, that's the thing. We don't know. *He* doesn't know."

"He doesn't know why he needs my help?"

"No...um, kind of. See, it's complicated. It's...he needs help finding something. But he's not sure why, and..."

"Am I making you nervous, Ms. Bridges? I can close my eyes. They're steely, I know."

"No." She smiled and seemed to relax a little. Shoulders lost some tension. "It's just, the situation is complex. *His* situation is complex, too. I'm only here on his behalf and I don't know the best way to articulate it. And...it'd really be much better if you spoke with him. It's not a matter for the police and it's not a matter for us, and so..." She shrugged and almost indicated me with her hands. "Does that make sense?"

"It does. You adumbrated my entire career. How soon?"

"Soon as you can."

"Tomorrow morning?"

She smiled. Not embarrassed. More like relieved. "That'd be great."

"Where?"

"His home, please. I'll write down the address."

She did. I almost whistled. As it happened, Ulysses lived

on my favorite street in Roanoke. This Ulysses fellow was hewing toward supernal.

I indicated the check. "How about I make this out for two hours of my time? Then we'll see."

"Yes, okay."

"Give me a hint, Ms. Bridges. About what I'm getting into. You said the situation is complex and so is his condition. How so?"

"To put it bluntly, Mr. August," she said. Took a deep breath. "He has a form of amnesia."

"Amnesia," I said.

Brilliant detectives always repeat stuff.

"He needs you to find something. A dog. But he doesn't know why. He forgot. In fact, he hates dogs. But for reasons that you'll discover, we both think the dog is important."

"A dog."

"Yes."

"An important one."

She nodded. Eyes a little wide. "Very. You'll see."

"Dogs usually aren't important."

"He agrees. But he writes 'Find the dog' in his journal every day and he doesn't know why. If it's a dog even a man with amnesia remembers, then maybe it is?"

"Artfully phrased." I didn't tell her, because it might sound perverse and lurid, but I was stimulated.

January 2nd. Looking good already.

2

That evening I made lasagna.

I used bacon and Italian sausage and ground beef. Also, and here was the kicker, I made the noodles out of mozzarella cheese and almond flour and cream cheese. No carbs that way, because my ineffable roommate was terrified of them.

Check that. Housemate. Not roommate.

We were evolving.

Kix rode in an ObiMama sling, strapped to my back. Was he too big for this? Probably. But I wanted to wring all the babyhood possible out of my son before sending him off to college.

He pointed at sizzling pans and shouted things.

You're burning the Italian sausage.

"Yes, I see."

Drain the ground beef, you maniac.

"I'll drain the beef but I'm keeping the bacon grease. It's good for you."

That cannot possibly be true.

He threw his bottle in protest. Good thing; he'd been banging it against my shoulders.

Pick that up.

"I'm not picking it up."

Pick that up this INSTANT.

Instead, I turned on jazz—Coltrane.

Sheriff Stackhouse arrived first, just after six. She wore official law enforcement garb today. Hard to make khaki look that alluring. Most days she looked like a soap opera star playing the role of sheriff. Tonight she looked like a soap opera star playing the role of an airplane crash survivor. Usually she kissed my cheek, which I enjoyed, but today she only squeezed my arm. Still nice. Without speaking she opened one of the bottles of wine she kept next to the fridge—red blends, under twenty dollars a bottle—poured herself a glass and sat on a leather couch in the living room and closed her eyes.

I slid two trays of lasagna into the oven. Started running hot water.

"On the bright side," I told Stackhouse. "You still look good."

"Not for much longer." Eyes remained closed. She undid her belt, winced and shifted for more comfort. Drank some wine. "I'm getting too old for this."

"Were you forced to shoot a hostage? That'd really ruin my day, I was you."

She half-smiled. "I don't mind the violence. It's the political maneuverings. Nothing but meetings with do-gooders, all of whom have the *best* ideas how to fix crime and also slash our budget."

"When you say *best*, do you mean—"

"I mean the worst ideas you can imagine."

"I was afraid you might."

Stackhouse said, "Free mental health care for the home-less. She's convinced all the local counselors will do the work pro bono. My ass."

Kix shouted for his bottle of juice. I put him in his playpen. He shouted some more. Adolescence starting early.

My old man Timothy August came next. Handsome guy, streaks of gray, could be a news anchor. All his hair, trust-worthy eyes. He entered without comment, same as his paramour. Tie already loose. He sat next to her, picked up her legs, and laid them across his lap. I brought him a glass of cabernet sauvignon—sixty dollars a bottle.

He took the glass. "I knew there was a reason we birthed you."

"Plus easing the burden of existential angst."

I changed the channel from the news to ESPN. No reason to release more pain and animus into the house.

Manny returned home soon, along with one of his co-workers, Noelle Beck. She was coming around more, though clearly proceeding on a platonic plank. Tall and trim. Light brown hair worn in a mousy bun, always. She wore black Rockports, a neat navy suit, no tie, white shirt buttoned all the way up. Good posture. Noelle was a Mormon, which came with dress code intransigencies I thought, but still I wished she spent an extra three minutes prepping in the morning. Thirty seconds for mascara and two and a half minutes for conditioner. Maybe Ronnie could teach her how a hair brush worked.

Manny on the other hand—such a handsome son of a gun it made my head hurt. Trim waist, broad shoulders, easy grace, quick smile, brilliant teeth, gah. Even Kix thought so. He shrugged out of his white sports jacket and greeted the room. The gun under his arm, the gun on his belt, and the tattoos on his arms caught the light and gleamed, which, I thought, was cool.

"Beck," I said. "Staying for dinner?"

"Mack, thanks," she said. She worked her phone in one hand but she glanced at Manny for permission. She wanted to. "I really can't stay though. Just dropping Manuel off." Their relationship was a peculiar one. Even Kix thought so.

"Stay. I made ambrosia."

"Of course Beck is staying, amigo," Manny announced. He opened the fridge door for a low carb beer. "Need to fatten her up."

"Why do you get to decide?" I said.

"Because I did."

"Do you set out her pajamas too? Enforce a strict bedtime?"

He paused, struck with epiphany. "Beck, you moisturize at night, *si?*"

Beck was on loan to Roanoke from the NSA. A computer wiz. Stupefied by his question, she paused, lowering into the corner reading chair. "Moisturize?"

"You work hard, señorita, chasing bad guys. Well, kinda. Gotta protect the skin."

"Like...with a cream?"

"*Ay dios mio.*"

"Manny, babe, maybe let me talk with the girl about this," Stackhouse said. "Just because you're pretty doesn't mean you're a woman."

He lowered the bottle of beer, the suction producing a soft pop. "What do you use?"

"Olay Advanced," said Stackhouse.

"That's for the *day*, mamí."

"I use it at night."

"Because we're still cave people?"

"What do you use?"

"Verso Night Cream."

"Verso?" Stackhouse sat up a little straighter. "You're joking. That's a hundred dollars a bottle."

"Look at this face. Find a wrinkle."

Beck offered, "I have some Burt's Bees stuff, I think, I could use."

"Burt's Bees? That's a toy for children, Beck! What, Mormons hate their complexion? You wanna look like Mack at his age?"

"Um," I said.

Stackhouse grinned. "What else, Manny? You and Agent Beck going to get breast implants?"

With his free hand, Manny pounded his chest. "Feel these pecs, señorita sheriff. Nothing but American muscle and testosterone and questionable supplements. But, Beck what bra size are you?"

Kix gasped.

"Good hell," said my father and he rubbed at his eyes. "How soon is dinner ready, son?"

"Not soon enough, that's for damn sure."

Stackhouse closed her eyes again. "I love this house and the people in it. Truly. I'd be a wreck without it."

Half an hour later we set the long table situated between the kitchen and the living room. Lasagna and garlic bread and caesar salad, wines and beers. Water for Beck. Juice for everyone under two.

Before we sat down, Veronica Summers entered. She arrives in a room the way Victoria Secret angels enter a runway—with verve and elegance and the wow factor. She didn't glow, but kinda. Today she wore a form-fitting khaki and black jacket combo, and black heels with red soles (which I'm told is important). She is tall, elegant but with feminine muscularity.

A month married to her and I still found things to admire. Yesterday it was a certain laugh she reserved solely for Kix. This morning I admired the curve of her jawline, especially as it curled under her ears. Her jaw looked stronger and more sinewy than most. I'd looked it up—she had great superficial masseter muscles, creamy skin tight across. I had yet to share this impossibly romantic compliment with her.

"Look at you people." She laid down her coat and bag. She smiled and we all corrected our posture. "So beautiful. Honestly, TLC needs to know about this house and the men who live here and the foolish women who totter after them."

I held up a flute of sparkling wine. "Freshly poured."

She took it, making sure her fingers brushed mine. "You read my mind. And the dishes are already washed? Should you and I run upstairs before dinner? Because...I'm ready."

"If you insist."

"No," said Stackhouse. "Sit, gorgeous. I'm starving. Be in love on your own time."

Ronnie went around the table kissing cheeks, including Beck's, who always got a little quiet around her. I knew the feeling.

I said grace. Not everyone shared my convictions about a personal and benevolent higher power, but they all felt grateful for our blessings. Which, I thought, hurt their case.

We ate.

Ronnie was worried. I'd learned the signs. This wasn't a major worry because no lines violated her forehead, but she had a far-off look. A small worry then.

I asked.

She said, "Not a big deal. We'll talk sometime when the lovely Sheriff can't eavesdrop."

Ah. That meant trouble in the underworld. She remained an active player. Now I was worried. But intrepidly so.

Ronnie asked after my day. I told her I'd been hired to talk with a guy who had amnesia about a lost dog.

"A dog," she said. And smiled again. I remained calm. "That's charming. What kind?"

"He can't remember. Nor can he remember why he wants it, because he hates dogs."

"Who could hate a dog? I had several growing up. Strays from the pound. My father wouldn't buy me a designer puppy."

"I always wanted one," I said.

"And never had one?" Ronnie loosed a scowl upon Timothy August. "No dogs? What was wrong with your parents?"

"Awful people," said Timothy. "Hated dog hair. Still do."

"What about a breed that doesn't shed? Like a Doberman?" asked Stackhouse. "I love a good Doberman. Bite the ass off a felon."

"Yes, but who'd clean up the feces?"

"Kix," I said.

Kix did not reply. Unbeknownst to us he'd fallen asleep in his chair. Head down and to the side, deep breaths making his forehead bob. His fingers still on his tray, gripping lasagna.

Ronnie had been prone to tears recently. Her eyes misted and she said, "Look at the perfect boy. He's so beautiful I could die. I'll put him to bed."

She got up and wiped his hands.

Beck dabbed at her mouth and nodded toward Manny.

"The Marshals could've used a doberman last week. Would save Sinatra a lot of running."

Ronnie paused.

I paused.

The tabled hushed.

Beck glanced at us, aware she'd said something amiss. Unsure what. She set down her fork.

I cleared my throat. "Would save...*who*...a lot of running?"

Beck reddened; her hands went to her mouth.

Manny aimed his finger at Beck and dropped his thumb. "Uh oh, Beck. Now I gotta shoot you."

Manuel Martinez was a US Marshal. But he was also something else. An operative for a domestic black ops team he couldn't discuss. This was the first specific detail I'd heard. Meant Beck was on the team too.

"Manny," I said. "Are you, pray, the Sinatra she refers to?"

Manny grinned. "Don't ask, don't tell, señor. But if I did have a secret code name? I would be named after one of the greatest Americans ever, that's for sure."

Stackhouse was laughing. "Sinatra? Really, babe?"

"Don't know why you're laughing. 'Cept maybe jealousy."

"Oh gosh." Beck still looked like a radish. "I should, I should go."

"Get some moisturizer on the way home. Wash your mouth out with soap. And think about all the ways you disappointed Uncle Sam today, *hermanita*."

"Do you outrank Beck?" I asked him.

"No," she said.

"Yes," he said. "Morally."

Ronnie got Kix free from his chair. "I'm putting this guy

to bed. And then, maybe, his father would like to join me upstairs?"

"He would."

"And bring the bottle of white wine too, please, oh husband of mine."

"I absolutely love this place," Stackhouse said, smiling into her glass of red.

3

Veronica Summers made a sigh. A sound of sleepy bliss. She turned over in bed and scooted her warm body closer to mine. I didn't protest. She buried her nose into my chest and made another happy noise when I draped my arm around her, hand at the small of her back. If heaven is real, and I believed that it must, many days would pass thusly.

"I'm not getting tired of this," she said. Eyes closed.

"Waking up with me?"

"Waking up with my husband."

"In a state of ethereality."

"Whatever that means. Should we go on another honeymoon?"

"By all means, though we never went on a first honeymoon."

"What do you call those three days we spent having wild sex in the Caribbean?"

"I call them empyrean," I said. "Wanna tell me what you're worried about? I deduce it involves your nefarious enterprises."

"Not yet. I'm too happy at the moment," she said.

"I deduced something else."

"Oh?"

"Your hair looks tidier now than it did last night, after our matrimonial recreation. And your breath smells minty. And your face is pink from being scrubbed."

"You private investigators. Can't you unplug?"

"My powers of detection inform me that you got up early again and freshened yourself in the bathroom."

She poked me in the ribs. "So?"

"So then you came back to bed, hoping I'd be duped into believing you wake up perfect. And by comparison, it makes me feel shabby."

"I want to look and feel pretty first thing in the morning. Sue me."

"I'll still like you. Even when your hair is a fright."

"I'd rather not risk it. Besides," she said. She got up on all fours and slid on top of me. Her chin rested on my chest. "I'm going to seduce you into a quickie before work and my chances are better if I don't look like Medusa."

My heart, the immodest romantic, skipped a beat. "But I haven't freshened up and I look like Erik, the disfigured Phantom of the Opera."

She smiled, a brilliant battering ram of a thing. "It doesn't matter what the man looks like. So try to enjoy yourself, Phantom."

And I did.

MY FAVORITE STREET in Roanoke is Robin Hood, halfway up Mill Mountain. Near Nottingham Road, which is just the most charming thing. Lots of towering oaks and pine, and the road frolics. Or maybe it meanders. Ivy everywhere, the kind thinking itself noble. Each house looks as though a zillionaire gave bags of cash to a different architect and said, "Go nuts, but make it classy."

Ulysses Steinbeck lived in a sprawling contemporary home set atop a wooded hill. A strong horizontal datum defined the roofline and a large array of picture windows offered the owner views in all directions. Also it was painted green. I parked in his drive behind an older Mercedes A-Class, walked up the brick path, and rang the doorbell.

Rose Bridges pulled open the double doors. She surprised me—she looked like a million bucks. Or at least she looked much more confident and comfortable than in my office. She was barefoot and had slender feet, good arches. Her shirt was pale blue with white stripes and a white collar, cuffed up to the elbows. Dainty golden pendant at her throat. Her hair was up in a bun, but a classy one, and her arms weren't crossed defensively.

There's no place like home.

She smiled. "Mr. August. I'm so glad."

"Me too."

"You're very tall, aren't you."

"If we played basketball, Rose, I'd probably win."

She laughed and waved me inside.

Ulysses Steinbeck sat in a study that could've been carved from one large block of rich mahogany. The book-shelves towered with tomes, the hardwood floor glinted, the ceiling had exposed rafters, and the windows behind gave a breathtaking view straight up the mountain. Oldies music played from an old fashioned radio in the corner. There was a wrought iron chandelier probably worth more than Kix.

The man at the desk watched me behind wire specta-cles. He didn't look like a man with amnesia. He looked like

a retired J. Crew model. The man had a cleft—a *cleft*—in his
chin. Not one perfect white hair had he lost. He wore a
turtleneck. I saw leather moccasin drivers under the table,
ankles crossed. Pale blue eyes.

I paused at the door. His eyes narrowed. Wondering.

"Ulysses, this is Mackenzie August," said Rose Bridges.
"He's going to sit with you until you're ready."

"Very good," he said.

I sat in the chair opposite.

He had three leather journals in front of him. Genuine
leather and sturdy, not the twenty dollar variety. Each was
branded with large letters. The first journal read, *Who is
Who*. The second journal, *Your History*. The third, *What is
Happening Right Now*.

"Mackenzie August," he said. Polite voice, a little
confused. He looked at the three journals. Selected the
What is Happening Right Now volume, opened it, and flipped
to the most recent page. Heavyweight paper. He ran his
finger down the side, skimming his elegant handwriting.
Today's date already took up a page and a half. He made a
hmm noise and spoke to himself under his breath.
Mumblings. "One moment...one moment," he said louder
for my benefit. "Need to refresh..."

"Sure."

He frowned over a few paragraphs, flipped back another
page. "Ah hah," he said. "Yes." His finger kept sliding down
the paper. He closed the book then and opened *Who Is Who*.
Flipped to the A's, and found my name. I couldn't read what
it said. "Okay. I'm up to speed, I think. You know about my
condition with short-term memories."

"I do. I'm impressed with your system to compensate."

He opened *What Is Happening Right Now* again and
began scribbling under today. "It's necessary. I was born

with an unusually active mind, and then I educated it thoroughly for thirty-five years, and now I refuse to let it atrophy simply because of anterograde amnesia."

"How long before your brain resets and you forget me? I know I'm not asking that correctly, but I'm curious if we need to rush."

He smiled like that pleased him. "An excellent question, Mr...August. My mind will not reset. As long as I stay on task and focus on you and this conversation, much of it will appear normal. As soon as we're finished or I get distracted, this will fade into fog. I cannot transfer the short-term into the long-term. But the immediate is functional."

Behind him, near the window, three chess sets were set up. I bet he played via snail mail. The only part of this room not dripping with prestige was a whiteboard in the corner covered with schedules and check marks and notes. On the chair next to the chess sets was today's newspaper, littered with pen scratching.

He noticed my gaze. "I do not trust modern technology. I remember that of myself perfectly well, and I still don't. Nothing beats pen and paper."

"The pen is mightier than the stylus?"

"Well phrased."

"You write all over the newspaper so you'll remember you read the article."

"Correct. And the notes jog my memory to some extent. You smell good, Mr. August." He flipped open *Who is Who* again and wrote under my name. I noticed he used a fountain pen with a fine gold nib. "That will help me. Olfactory input nudges the mind. Would you mind wearing it if we meet again?"

"It's Prada. A pretty girl got it for me in Italy."

He arched an eyebrow.

I shrugged. Tried to look modest. "She says I'm worth it."

"You look as though you played football. In college?"

"In fact I did. We lost a lot."

With his pen, he pointed at my head. "Any residual effects? From concussions?"

"Not yet."

"What do you know about me?"

"Almost nothing," I said. "Only that you want me to find your dog."

"Dog," he said as if I reminded him. "Yes. Let's begin. Here's the short version of my history. I was traumatically injured in a car crash. My memory is crystalline up until maybe two months before the crash. Ever since, I live in a fog. Tomorrow, if we meet, it'll be like our conversation today didn't happen and I'll rely on my notes to catch me up."

"You don't know the details of your crash?"

"They are forgotten." He patted the *History* journal. "I'm positive it's in here, or in one of the previous volumes I'm sure I preserve, but I don't want to look. Just the thought causes me emotional distress."

"You are entirely reliant on your journals? Which means, you are entirely reliant on your thoroughness yesterday."

"Exactly phrased." Again he appeared pleased. I'm so smart. He scratched notes as we spoke. "If I write down a lie, it would be disaster. If I quit writing today, tomorrow's version of myself would suffer. This is one of the facts foremost in my mind that does not fade into the fog. More of an operational memory, which I do not lose—the journaling and the necessity of it."

"What did you do before the accident?"

"I was a radiologist. Still am. I did not lose my ability to diagnose disease from image studies. I wake up most mornings convinced it's time for work, though quickly I realize I no longer practice full-time. I see by the board over your shoulder," he said, pointing at a whiteboard behind me I hadn't noticed. I twisted to look. "That already this week two hospitals sent pictures my way for a third opinion. But, you understand, I cannot be the primary opinion on any case." According to the board, today he'd eaten breakfast but not lunch. "Anyway, we digress. As you adroitly noted I'm entirely dependent on my notes, which are produced by me but originate from knowledge and facts I've forgotten."

I nodded.

I was adroit. As heck.

"In some ways, it's like I'm following the whims of a man I never met. I have no choice but to trust that he is honest and good. Which brings us to the reason for your visit. Take a look at this, Mr. August." He consulted with *What is Happening Now*, flipped backwards to a page in *History*, and spun it so I could see. Most pages were taken up with several dozen lines of script. But the bottom half of this page simply read, **Find the dog. The dog is the key. Do NOT ignore.** "Scanning backwards from today, it appears that every day I write down the page number for this note. Find the dog."

"What dog?"

"I don't know. But some inner part of my brain thinks it's important."

"How long ago was the original note written?"

He tapped the date with his finger and consulted the white board. "Three years. Not long after the car crash, I believe."

"Why didn't you look for the dog then?"

"I...don't remember."

"Right."

He pulled the *History* journal back and closed it. He kept *What is Happening Now* open. He scanned more, as one does a jumbled puzzle. "Look here. Two days ago, I wrote that Rose says she'll help me remember to find the dog again. The phrase *again* is indicative. It means I tried before but failed."

"You remember Rose? Every day?"

He smiled and looked up at the doorway, though she wasn't there. "Rose is a lifesaver. She was my housekeeper before the accident. So yes." He kept tapping the note about Rose promising to help him remember the dog. "My past self left no further clues. So...I'm trusting *him* that this is worthwhile. Think of the dog as an itch I need to scratch, but most of the time I don't pay it much attention. Even so, satisfying the need will bring a measure of peace. But I need an able-bodied and able-minded person to do so. In my notes, you are listed as competent and trustworthy from a source I respect."

"Okay. I'll find the dog."

"Excellent, thank you."

"What then?"

He shrugged. Almost looked dismayed. "I don't know."

"I bet you don't often get bored."

"You're right. The whole day feels like a revelation. Tomorrow will be the same, I imagine."

"While I look, your job is to determine what to do once I find it."

He didn't reply.

"Let me hazard a guess. I have to find the dog without reading through your journals."

He nodded. "Yes. These are as precious and private to me as are your own inner thoughts and emotions."

"Except," I pointed out. "I remember my thoughts and

emotions. Whereas you have to worry about secrets you don't know exist."

"Precisely. Mr. August, let me congratulate you on your adaptability and perception. I retain a vague frustration with people's inability to cope or understand my limitations. You work around it naturally."

"Well," I said. And shrugged. Brilliance being par for the course.

"Rose will provide you with a check."

"Are there budgetary limitations?"

"Um," he said. He placed his hands on the journals. Thought a moment. Glanced at both white boards. Said, "You know, I'm not positive. I used to be rich. I still work. So...I doubt it?"

"I'll ask her."

"Perfect," he said again and he wrote in his journal.

ROSE and I drank tea in the gourmet kitchen. I had a kitchen like this, I'd have two Michelin stars by now.

She blew into her china cup, the kind with thin blue designs. "Budgetary limitations, Mr. August? I don't know how to answer. I keep his checkbook, so... Can you keep it under twenty-five thousand dollars?"

I did not spill my tea. "I can."

"Good."

"Tell me about him. I need a place to start."

"Oh, yes, I'll try.

"You know him well, I assume."

She nodded. "I've worked for Ulysses seven years, including the three since the crash. First as a housekeeper, then as a caretaker. He's lived here for maybe fifteen?"

"Anything I should know about the car wreck?"

She looked unhappy. "He drove off a short cliff. Late at night, he was exhausted. No other cars involved."

"Family?"

"He is divorced. Happened around the time of his accident."

"That have anything to do with the car crash?"

She set down her mug. Didn't look at me. "I hope not."

"Where does the ex-wife live?

"Here, in Roanoke. I'll write down the address."

"Any children?"

"Yes. A daughter. The great joy of his life. That's her there." She indicated a framed photo near the light switches. Blonde girl smiling next to an Audi with a big red bow on it. "Alex is at Virginia Tech. I'll get you her number."

"Any idea which dog he wants to find?"

"I have an educated guess. He bought a puppy a month before his accident. That's the only dog he's ever been around, as far as I can tell. After the crash, we lost her."

"Has he previously tried finding it?"

"Yes. It's difficult to search for long when you can't remember what you're looking for. Or why. The police laughed us off. A year ago he hired a different private investigator and, well..."

"You had a bad experience."

"We did."

"He took your money and a week later said he'd looked everywhere and couldn't find anything," I said.

"Yes. That's what happened."

"Which is why you looked nervous in my office."

"I did?"

"Who was he?"

She told me. I knew the guy—a clown. I said, "Understandable. This time will be different, Rose."

She looked like she wanted to be relieved, like she wanted to believe me. "That's what we heard."

"Would Ulysses remember about the dog if it wasn't for the journal?"

"I think so. It nags at him, vaguely. He doesn't remember details, but ideas and...themes get lodged. And recently, he's waking up preoccupied with something and when he looks at his notes he remembers that it's the dog. And then remember it again later in the day. I know that's weird."

"Tell me about the puppy."

"He brought the dog home just before the accident. A puppy. But he hated dogs, Mr. August. Isn't that strange? It had been wounded somehow at the breeder, but quickly recovered. Then, after the accident, one day it was gone."

"What kind of dog?"

"A boxer."

"Short hair," I said.

"Yes. He hated dog hair. Even so, the puppy was a great surprise."

"What kind of wound?"

"I don't know. It healed quickly, but perhaps seeing the wound stirred his paternal instincts?"

"His journal said the dog was the key. To what?"

She picked up her tea cup. "I don't know."

"Have you checked the pounds? I imagine they keep records."

"I assume the previous man we hired tried? But, Mr. August, I don't think the puppy simply ran away. It was a *puppy,* and I had to pay her close attention. Remember, he got it just weeks before his accident. While he was in the hospital, I moved in here and I took care of the dog and house at the request of his family. When he came home, he had a nurse tend the burns and check his vitals, and an occupational therapist help with memory loss coping strategies, and he had other visitors. In and out, in and out. And it was during this time that the puppy, well, it vanished. She had a collar, so I don't think...I mean, if she ran away or was hit by a car, we'd have been notified."

"So," I said with keen perspicaciousness. "Someone took it."

"Maybe? I think so."

"Why'd you move in?"

"The family asked me to."

"What's the dog's name?"

"Georgina Princess Steinbeck."

"Jiminy Christmas."

"It's a lot." She said it with a laugh.

"For a man who hated dogs."

"Yes. Isn't it silly?"

"So, the dog, the divorce, and the car wreck. They all happened...what, within a month?"

She looked as though she wanted to cry. "He got a dog, he wrecked, and the divorce finalized three days after he returned home from the hospital—in that order. His ex-wife isn't a heartless woman, though. That's simply the way it played out."

"Was the divorce contentious?"

"A little. He...well, he squandered much of their money when they separated. Very out of character for him, and she was understandably upset."

"Yikes."

"It was a hard time for everyone. Especially their daughter, Alex."

I said, "Can you generate a list of everyone who visited him around the time the dog disappeared?"

"I'll try. It was three years ago, however."

"The details are hazy."

"Hazy, yes." She nodded into her tea.

"That's how he feels, I bet. All the time."

"Oh. What a very clever point, Mr. August."

"There are many kinds of stupidity, Rose, and I'm afraid cleverness is the worst."

"You're quoting someone?"

"Yes," I said. "But botching it."

4

I was married. Technically. Kinda. My marriage had been imparted to me.

I was married to a prostitute. Or, she had been. Kinda. Against her will.

It was complex.

But she quit the lifestyle and angered people. The people were angry at her and angry at me. And angry at their parents for rearing them in such a way they'd become reliant on prostitutes for affection. She asked for our phones to be linked so I could see her location at all times. She got kidnapped, I'd know immediately. Not a bad idea. Creepy, but not bad.

Long way of saying, I knew she was at her office because a map on my phone told me so. I called Roxanne and asked her to keep Kix an extra hour, and I drove to Veronica's office, off Salem Avenue downtown Roanoke, and nestled into the long galley parking lot among the panoply of lower tier luxury cars. She worked on the second floor of a reno-vated brick building with several law offices, great view of the trains.

Her receptionist was gone for the day.

Ronnie sat at her desk. If angels could look weary, that'd be her expression. She saw me and smiled and I didn't levitate but almost.

My old pal Ruben Collier took his ease across from her, his appearance incongruent with the upscale decor—he wore muddy work boots, Dickies, thick Carhartt jacket, unadorned ball cap, knife clipped inside his pocket. Large eyes, friendly smile.

"Ruben, you ol' prolific grower of marijuana, you." We shook hands. Mine were stronger. His were tougher. Call it a tie. "How's business."

He grinned good-naturedly. "S'the winter, Mr. August. I'm recuperating. Bout to take the wife to Florida for a week."

"Rubes, can I call you Rubes? Rubes, what'll happen when the entire nation legalizes weed? You go out of business? Or start making even more?"

"Got no idea. After all, ain't my business. It's hers." He nodded at Veronica Summers, my wife. Kinda.

Veronica blew a strand of blond hair away from her face. "That's what we're discussing."

"Trouble afoot? Other than you producing and distributing enough 'Schedule I' narcotics to go to prison forever?"

She groaned and laid her head on the desk. "Yes. Other than that. One of my wholesale buyers was arrested."

"You have wholesale buyers?"

"Apparently."

Ruben Collier said, "He's gone. Prison for the next twenty years."

"Can he rat on either of you?"

"No. Everything I handled was through drop-offs and

the phone, Mr. August. Trouble is, I got bushels of weed just a'sitting there."

"Sorry, bushels?"

He nodded. "Bushels, Mr. August."

Ronnie groaned. Head down, she gripped a pen in both hands and absently twisted. "I don't want to sell marijuana. Or grow it, or whatever. Even if it makes me rich."

"Does it make you rich?"

She raised up. Eyes wide. Slow nod. "More than I make as an attorney. A lot more. And I love being rich. But still, I don't wanna."

"So crime *does* pay. I suspected it might. Maybe Ruben would like to own the land he tends? And the inherent business?"

"Oh no." He raised his hands, palms out. "No sir, not for me. I like things the way it is."

"Ruben is helping me brainstorm. We need to move the marijuana. A lot of dealers south of here are without product. Unhappy buyers and unhappy dealers, but we don't know who they are or how to contact them. Only my wholesaler knew them. It's all run through relationships. But apparently," she said and she pointed at Ruben. "They know how to contact Ruben. And they're making threats."

I said, "So send them the bushels."

"We've heard from two dealers so far. But I bet there are...I don't know, dozens? Hundreds? Waiting and angry? I don't want to anger the Kings either. They get a small cut, I think. This is a mess, Mackenzie."

Ruben winked at me. "See? I don't want to be in charge, sir."

"Where are the bushels now?"

"Got'em in a climate controlled storage unit, Franklin County."

"Ruben, you're the tops."

"Anything worth doing, Mr. August, better do it right. Even if I can tell you don't approve of her being in the business."

"Okay." Ronnie stood. Set her hands on the table and leaned on them. "I'm tired. Let's make a decision. Here's what it is. Ruben, thank you for letting me know. I'll have answers for you within a couple days. Mackenzie, you're taking me to dinner. I need alcohol and maybe lobster. And then we're arranging a meeting with Marcus. I bet he knows a buyer. Maybe he'll buy me out himself. Sound good to everyone?"

Ruben chuckled and nodded. "Absolutely, Ms. Summers."

I nodded also. "Absolutely, Ms. Summers."

～

WE ATE AT TABLE 50. She ordered low country shrimp and grits—not lobster, which was overrated anyway. She didn't eat much but it looked good next to her two dirty martinis. I had a rack of lamb with polenta and a Fat Tire. The lights were down, the candles lit, the waiters pious. Our table was in the corner, giving us freedom to wholly express ourselves.

"Mackenzie, would it hurt your feelings if I slept at my place tonight?"

"It would not."

"That's one of your many baffling characteristics." She ate a shrimp thoughtfully. "You aren't easily offended. Or offended at all."

"The world needs fewer people getting offended, you ask me. Love is patient. And does not take offense."

"Most of the girls I know use taking offense as a tool to manipulate. Are these girls not in love?"

I drank some beer. "Doing their best at it. Failing a lot. Love is not an easy thing to do. Are you such a girl?"

"I'll try not to be. It will require practice. But, about tonight, life has been a whirlwind. I'm behind on work and I haven't been home recently even though that's where all my beautiful clothes are, and...and I think there might be two girls still living there. I forgot about them."

"Prostitutes?"

"Whores, prostitutes, call girls, whatever they are, yes. But, no, I just remembered, they left last week. That's good. I miss my bed."

"Two prostitutes you're rescuing?"

"You can't rescue people, Mackenzie. You taught me that. I gave them a safe place for a while."

I said, "You're doing a lot."

"It *is* a lot." She nodded. She wielded her fork to delicately slide a shrimp into the pile of grits. Slid it out and pushed it in again, not watching. She looked out of place here, as though the ambiance hit her differently than us mortals. She carried movie star lighting with her. Her articulation made me realize I mumble, her posture made me realize I slouch. "And it all happened so fast. My father dying, the showdown with Darren, your abduction, the trip to Italy, your recovery..."

"Not to mention our sudden and unexpected marriage."

"Right." She smiled. "That was a larger surprise for you than me. Do you think we should get it annulled?"

"Maybe."

She sucked in air. Dropped her fork. Knocked over her empty martini glass. The candles caught in her eyes, turning a shade of hurt. "Oh. Oh wow, I didn't..."

"Hear me out."

"Oh Jesus, I was just joking. You want...?"

I placed my hands on hers. Squeezed so she couldn't pull away. "Ronnie. Relax. What I meant was, I never got to propose. We didn't do it right."

Her fingers trembled.

I said, "One of the things about me, I keep my word. I keep promises. And we never made them."

She nodded. Not looking at me. "Okay. So then...so?"

"I think we should."

"You want to have a real wedding ceremony? Me in a white dress?" She snorted. "Walk down the aisle, throw flowers, eat fucking cake?"

"I couldn't care less about ceremonies and flowers. But the vows seem important. And the cake."

She nodded. Still shaken and unconvinced.

Mackenzie August, leaping before he looks.

"Ronnie—"

"I switched counselors," she said. Eyes on the candle. Resembling a lost, scared teenager girl. "Total Life Counseling."

"Like it?"

"I confessed everything. In the first thirty minutes, I mean, I just... I told her I killed my dad. Told her I killed a woman in Italy. That somehow I'm the biggest marijuana producer in western Virginia. Used to be a prostitute. It simply spilled out. She was very kind. As she listened, she grew pale. She started perspiring and drank an entire bottle of water. She prescribed anti-anxiety meds. Recommended we meet next week, and often thereafter. On her note pad, I bet she wrote, 'Bitch is a hopeless mess.'"

"That is some elite psychotherapy jargon."

"My point is, Mackenzie, I'm a wreck. I cover it up well with mascara, but...it's there."

"I think—"

"And you know what? You are too. A wreck, I mean."

I nodded. "No question. For example I'm late picking up my son."

"No, I mean it. For a long time, I thought you were a whole human being. The most complete person I knew. But...you aren't, are you."

"Sooner you realize that the better."

"I phrased that incorrectly. You're still the best person I know, I think. I still adore you. But you have a significant character flaw."

I frowned. "Okay. Easy. Flaw is a little harsh. I have...creases."

"Want to know what your character flaw is?"

"Heavens no."

"You're dedicating yourself to the wrong woman. And you can't stop."

I didn't reply. We proceeded on thin ice and I detected deepening cracks. Everybody be cool. Also, Lancelot though I may be, I didn't like my flaws highlighted.

"You work so hard to keep your home perfect," she said. "That's the place of order, and you leave the orderliness to step into chaos and subdue it. See, Mackenzie? I listen to your vernacular. But the problem is, you brought the chaos home with you. Me."

"You."

"Yes. It's a grand slam for me. And fun for you. Until I destroy it. You can't save me. You know that. But you don't believe it."

I leaned back in my chair. Resettled my napkin. Drank some beer.

We watched one another. The air hummed with silence.

"It hasn't occurred to you," I said, "that perhaps I'm with you for selfish reasons?"

"It has. It is selfish of you to feed your sense of nobility." She closed her eyes. A line formed in her forehead. "Wow, Christ, that came out poorly."

"I keep you around because you make me happy. That is a selfish act. Were I noble as I think I am, I would only do it for your benefit. But I'm as enamored with you as most men are. I am possessive and self-indulgent and frightened, even when I try not to be."

Her eyes were still closed. The candle light dappling shifted across her shirt as she took deep breaths. "I go to counseling for you. Because I know I should. To change. But deep down, I know I'm organically the wrong person. You shouldn't be with me."

"Because in a romantic comedy or novel, you would be the wrong woman? The nasty seductress the hero rejects at the end, turning his affections instead onto the charming and innocent heroine, and the crowd applauds?"

"Don't make it sound cute."

"Ronnie. You went to Italy for me. Risked your life. You spent untold thousands of dollars. You shot a woman because she sexually assaulted me."

Her eyes opened. The right corner of her lips curled. "I did do that."

"I know you're a volcano. A volcano with seismic shifting. But...I like the way you look in jeans."

She laughed. A sudden sound, perhaps my favorite. "I can't promise this ends well for you, Mackenzie. Even if I'm hopelessly in love with you."

"That's what the vows are for. You *have* to promise me that."

"Oh." She paused. Searched my face thoughtfully. "Oh. That's...revelatory. I never thought of vows like that before."

"Because you're in the business of writing legal contracts, you think of a marriage that way. A legal contract easily voided down the road. That's not what I'm after."

"The way you describe it makes the vows so much more...personal and intimate. Staggeringly important."

"Yes."

"So...sure, that's great. And beautiful. Yet." She squeezed my hand. We were touching the entire time. "Not everyone has your sense of duty. Your scruples. Marriage vows are broken every day."

"It's a leaky boat. But it's the one holding the most water, I think. Our best chance."

"Mackenzie, being very honest, you still don't know how broken I am inside. Vows don't provide protection from... from volcanoes."

I nodded. "You've been raped and abused for twenty years. You're a wreck. I know this. But...sometimes the heart wants what it wants."

"You like me just because you do."

"The reasons are accruing, I admit."

"Do you know, Mackenzie," she said, releasing my hand and waving for the check. "You have never told me you love me."

I nodded.

She said, "Don't say it yet. I admit it, your idea is good. We need a ceremony and to officially exchange vows. You can tell me then. Because I'm realizing saying you love me would be making a promise. And you take that seriously."

"I do."

"Maybe I shouldn't sleep at my place tonight."

"Worried you'll lose me?"

"Possibly. I've never had something of value before. I've never worried about losing someone."

I said, "Fret not. I am yours."

"Also, what happens if I become prurient?"

"Abstinence makes the heart grow fonder."

5

I visited the Roanoke SPCA and the local Angels of Assisi, inquiring after Georgina Princess Steinbeck. At both establishments I spoke with a woman—shouted actually.

"Loud," I told the woman at the SPCA, in case she'd grown inured to the baying of the hounds from cages.

The woman replied, "They're just excited about the new day, that's all."

"They'll continue without surcease?"

"Pretty much, whatever the hell surcease means." She typed into the computer some more. Her wrists had claw marks from cats. Also, so did her face. Stupid cats. "Tell me the name again?"

I did.

"Exotic and self-indulgent, no?"

She said, "You kidding? Met a dog last week named Mamma's Lost Cause. Got a cat in the back, collar says Empress Pickle Juice. When did you say?"

I gave her the date, three years ago.

She frowned at the screen. "Nope. No boxers either, of

any name. Wish I could help find your dog, but that's a long time ago."

"Not my dog, actually."

"Oh. What kind you have?" She squinted. "Let me guess, I'm good at this. You're a black lab kinda guy."

"I'm not allowed. Dog hair, you know."

"Not allowed? To what?"

"To own a dog."

She stared at me. Couldn't find the words to express her disappointment. That I, a grown man, maybe, didn't own a dog. Or that I wasn't allowed to.

I cleared my throat. "I am humiliated."

"Naw, that's okay. Wish my husband listened to all my rules that way."

"Not my wife's rules. My father's. We still live...you know, I'm just gonna leave."

And I did, tail between my legs.

From the car I called some of the names on the list provided by Rose Bridges. Five people visited Ulysses Steinbeck soon after he returned from the hospital. That she could remember. Potentially one of them stole the animal.

I left a message for Stephanie Larson, a former colleague of his.

I reached Victor Simpson, the neighbor. Gruff man but loquacious, waxing eternally about Ulysses, a damn shame, also his ex-wife, a kind woman, the way a woman ought to be, a damn shame, don't remember the dog though, damned strange, why'd Ulysses have a dog?

Got me, Victor.

The next name on the list I knew. Dr. Whitney Potter, local pediatrician. She lived near Ulysses on Tradd, smoked a lot of dope. We'd once attended a swinger's party, full of intrigue and peril. At least for me; I'd nearly given up the ghost before being purchased by Veronica Summers. I liked Whitney, so I decided to swing by her office off McClanahan.

I stood in the waiting room surrounded by sneezing toddlers, crying babies, and tired women on their phones. A television in the corner had Sesame Street. The walls were decorated with laminated posters of cartoon characters with minor injuries and catchy warnings about washing hands. The community toy box glistened with germs.

Whitney Potter herself escorted a family out from the examination area. She wore linen pants, the obligatory white jacket and stethoscope, and cute emoji necklace. Her hair was still a short pixie cut.

She saw me, pointed at my face with her finger, and crooked the finger to beckon. I obeyed. We went into the first empty patient room. She depressed a nozzle that dispensed cleaning solution, scrubbed the foam into her hands, and grabbed mine with hers.

"Mackenzie August, my favorite private detective, I need details. Gimme all of them before my next patient," she said.

I grinned. "You refer to my ongoing and torrid love affair with Ronnie Summers."

"Through the grapevine I heard she's sleeping at your place. When last we spoke, you two hadn't done anything worth writing a steamy novel about. Spill. I need it."

"We're married." Kinda.

"That's a shame. You're both off the market then. But, when and where—tell about the first time. Quickly, because I need to stick a tongue depressor down another kid's throat."

"It's better than you think."

Her grip tightened around my fingers. "Don't tease me."

"It was on a plane."

She closed her eyes. Released a throaty noise. "Shut up. That *is* better. Go on."

"A private jet. I was injured and not moving well. Only through her wonder and magic was the deed accomplished."

Had I been one ounce less a man, her grip would've been painful. "Go on. What were you wearing?"

"That's all you get."

"Mackenzie. I am a sexual deviant," she said.

"I know this."

"This moment we're in, this is the best moment of my week."

"How's Paul?"

"Paul's wondering if he should leave me. I won't tell him, but he'd be much happier if he did."

I said, "I'm hired by Ulysses Steinbeck."

"You're kidding. I know Ulysses."

"Intimately?"

"No. Nor his wife. They never attended. Hired to do what?"

"Find his dog."

She frowned. Glanced at her watch. "He got a dog? I'm surprised."

"He had one briefly. Three years ago. Lost it within a week, right around the time he returned from the hospital."

"You know, Mackenzie, that's funny. I suddenly remember it. A puppy, I think. Cute as hell. You're trying to find a dog from three years ago?"

"Yes. A glamorous life I lead. Any idea what happened to the dog?"

"No. How would I?" She stuck her head out of the door and called, "Sue, send the next one."

"As the divorce finalization neared, he got a dog and wrecked his car. Eldritch coincidences, right?"

"What on earth does eldritch mean?"

"Weird or sinister."

"Not weird. Tragic. A nightmare. Poor guy. Paul and I were so torn up. You chasing clues? Here's some gossip, how I love the stuff. Ulysses and Colleen drifted apart. Colleen, his wife. Ex-wife. Nothing awful, just people going in different directions. Rumors were they both found someone else and the divorce was amiable. I don't know about him, but I know about Colleen; she *had* found someone else. Gym guy, lots of muscles. Total beefcake. Kinda like you. They married so quickly we all assumed they'd been carrying on before. If Ulysses was with someone, she faded away immediately after the accident, the bitch."

"Could the ex-wife have gotten the dog somehow?"

"Jeez, Mackenzie, I dunno. Yeah, it's possible. They're still on speaking terms." A little kid and his mom came back. The mom shot me a second look. "Hey Chaz! Stick another marble up your nose? Mackenzie, we'll talk later? Maybe over some wine? On my back porch? Bring your wife. Pretty please."

I smiled.

No chance.

6

That evening it was just the August boys—Timothy, Kix, and me. Everyone else had obligations so we fried quesadillas with extra cheese and dipped them into homemade salsa. Kix glared piously at the salsa and refused it. He wanted a cookie, though, which meant he had to eat all his cheese and apples.

Near the end of dinner, the point at which humans grow philosophical, Timothy August said, "Strange, only the three of us. Makes one realize how large a percentage of words the women contribute."

I set down my bottle of Oak Barrel Stout. "Don't forget the Argentinian. Or Puerto Rican or whatever he is."

"Sinatra, you mean. Can never forget him." He set down his wine glass and indicated my hand. "Your electrical burns healed nicely."

I flexed my fingers. "The burns from Naples. Skin's tight in a few places. No real pain."

"Remember our deal. I don't ask questions, you don't offer answers or details about Italy. There are some things a father doesn't want to know."

"The reality can't be as bad as what your imagination cooked up."

"Still."

With my chin I nodded at the book he'd set down on the reading chair. "That Jordan Peterson I see?"

"Yes. His book on rules for living. You read it?"

"Sure."

"Of course you have," he said with kind of a snort. "You read everything. What'd you think?"

"I mostly read it so I'd sound learned and erudite at dinner parties."

"And?"

"He's fearless. Argues well. I was compelled. We disagree on some things."

"Like what?" asked my father.

"For example, his definition of existence or *being*. Under his definition, God doesn't exist. God is not compatible with Jordan's view on suffering or limitations or becoming."

Dad shook his head. Drank some beer. "You theologians. Way over my head. I'm still on the first chapter," he said. "About confidence and strength. So don't ruin it."

I took our dishes to the sink. Came back and picked up the beer again. "I could use some advice on Ronnie."

"I'll try," he said. "It'll be pagan and worldly advice, though."

"She thinks I have a serious character flaw. Essentially, I stick to things I shouldn't and one of them is her."

"Is she right?"

"Maybe. On paper we're a disaster. If I wasn't me, I'd warn myself about the eminent relational eruption."

"What's the Bible say?" he asked.

"Bible agrees with her. People shouldn't be unequally yoked."

"You two are oxen?"

I nodded sagely. "The best oxen."

"So if you agree with her and the Bible agrees with her..." He spread his hands, palms up like, *Need we go on?*

"She went to Italy for me. Risked everything."

Kix said some sweet things about how great he thought Ronnie was and I reward him with more chunks of apple.

Dad said, "I'm not counseling you two to break up, son. But are you with her out of obligation?"

"No."

"Are you with her to prove something to yourself?"

"...No. At least not entirely."

"Are you trying to save her?" he asked.

"...No. At least not entirely. I'm with her for a lot of reasons, most of them selfish. But she's got me thinking. Statistically recovering prostitutes almost always return to that lifestyle. It's a hard habit to break. She's got more baggage than most and so the odds of her being free of that *habit* aren't good. If she goes back we can't be together, clearly. And, sticking with oxen metaphor, we're animals accustomed to traveling at different speeds and moving in different directions. Suddenly yoked, it'll be hard soon. One will pull the other, probably resulting in anger and scorn on both sides. Pull hard enough, the yoke breaks and both oxen are wounded and maybe worse off than before."

He nodded. Thought a moment. He went for more wine and came back and resettled. "I'm trying to think of a more intelligent way to say this, but I can't. You just described marriage. People never married think it's easy. Anyone married knows the truth. Two people traveling at different speeds learning to co-exist in close quarters. You described it well."

"Isn't the point of dating or courtship or arranged

marriages to pair yourself as closely as possible with an ox heading your direction at your speed? To reduce the odds of a disaster?"

"Ideally, I think. But," he said and chuckled. "That way sounds like it'd be a boring sex life."

"Ew, Dad."

"Opposites attract and all that. Think about me and Stackhouse."

"I will not. This conversation has derailed."

Kix laughed and threw his bottle.

I said, "I don't want to be with anyone else."

"But you recognize that other women might be more suitable? That is to say, a more likeminded ox to be yoked with?"

"That book you're reading by Peterson, one of his rules is 'Compare yourself to who you were yesterday and don't compare yourself to other people.' She's evolving. Ronnie and I are a better match as time goes on. We're more suitable today than yesterday. Right?"

Timothy said, "I don't have the answers. No one does. Well, maybe God if he exists. Here's the thing about marriage—it's difficult. It's messy and hard and no one yokes perfectly. It's a fight, no other way around it."

I nodded. We stayed quiet a moment. Kix ate his final piece of apple and expressed his need for a reward.

Timothy said, "I haven't helped, have I."

"I was never looking for firm answers. I wanted to advance the ball up the field and I think we did."

"How so?"

"You confirmed my suspicions that modern romance is a fiction Hollywood sells. But I don't know where that leaves me."

Kix reached far enough to pat my hand. Smiled.

You'll figure it out, you big dummy. Now about the promised cookie?

7

Colleen Gibbs was the ex-wife of Ulysses. After the divorce, she'd fled—abandoning Roanoke City and traveling all the way to Roanoke County. Miles and miles apart, six in fact, to the estates around Hidden Valley Country Club.

I pulled into her drive. She and her new husband lived in a brick colonial house. Stately, two stories, black shutters, white trim, no windows on the sides. Lots of mulch, no shrubs. The brick walkway led straight to the door, no porch. My appearance surprised her husband—he'd been about to slide into his enormous yellow Hummer H2.

Probably bringing fresh supplies to the warfront with that thing.

I got out of my car. He noticed. Watched suspiciously. "Help you?"

"I'm looking for Colleen Gibbs."

"I'm Gordon Gibbs."

"Ah! You probably know her then," I said. Helpfully. Our words produced a little steam in the cool morning air.

Gordon was a beefcake—an overly tan one. He wasn't

lean and dense like he did CrossFit, he was heavily muscled like he did steroids. Shoulders the size of a spare tire. Kinda guy who screamed during bench presses and claimed The Rock was a weenie. He wore track pants and white Nikes and an Under Armour windbreaker. The pants and the jacket were black with white lettering. His head was shaved, like with a Gillette.

He said, "You're selling something."

"I am not, though."

"Why the hell are you in my drive? Move on."

"If I was selling something, could I stay?"

"What?"

"Colleen home?"

"Why?"

"I'm taking a survey."

"What?"

He realized he had repeated questions. Glowered.

I said, "Colleen home?"

He came around his modest yellow war tank and stopped near me, hands in his pockets. My Honda Accord scoffed at his tank for reasons of gas mileage and practicality. "Who wants to know?"

"Me. Obviously," I said. He stood taller than me, which isn't easy, and he was much wider, which is silly.

"Listen. Stop being an ass. You're at my house. Tell me what you want or take off."

"I want. To talk. To Colleen Gibbs. Maybe sign language would help."

"Why?" he said. I wasn't terrified of his bulk and I was toying with him verbally. He saw it. So he decided to thwart me with his own words. Zounds. "Tell me why. You don't understand the word why? Tell me why."

"Are you quoting the Backstreet Boys song? Remember

it? Tell me why, ain't nothing but a heartbreak. Tell me why, ain't nothing but a mistake. Right?"

He took his hands out of his pockets.

"Colleen home?" I asked. Winningest smile.

I thought his teeth might actually be grinding. "Who. Wants. To. Know?"

"Me. Jeez, Gordon we've been over this."

"Get out." He pointed.

"I'm not in."

Good *grief* I can be childish. Mackenzie August, major league pain in the neck. I needed to grow up.

I changed the subject, before he had an aneurism. "Do you have a dog?"

"Do I have...none of your business, asshole. Now go."

"I'm looking for the dog belonging to Ulysses Steinbeck. Thought I'd ask Colleen about it."

Some of the bunched muscles in his shoulders relaxed. "Ulysses? That stupid asshole? What for?"

"Do you call everyone asshole?"

"Just those who deserve it," he said.

"Ulysses does? I'm surprised. He struck me as congenial and affable. Do you need those defined?"

"Are you a relative of his? And no, I know what those words mean."

"No you don't," I said.

"Yes I do."

"Define them. I'll give you five bucks."

"Hey buddy, I'm Gordon Gibbs. You know the name? I don't play games with losers like you."

"Would you describe yourself as affable?" I asked.

"I—"

"Careful, Gordon. Don't want to insult yourself."

He shoved me. I took a step backwards. "How about I

kick your ass. Police wouldn't lift a finger. My property, I can do what I want."

"In fact you cannot. Nothing about what you said is accurate. In any of the three sentences. Hey Gordon, Colleen home?"

We both heard his front door open.

A woman's voice. "What's going on? Gordon, who's this?"

I replied, "We're comparing genital girth. He just surrendered."

The woman laughed. A little. Like maybe I had special needs.

I said, "In fact, I'm being a childish and major league pain in the neck to poor Gordon, who was merely trying to protect his home with the tenacity of a miniature poodle. I regret my verbal bullying."

"You can't bully me," he said. "I'm—"

"Gordon Gibbs, yes. It's enough to scare me to death. I'd like to talk with you, Colleen, about Ulysses."

"Ulysses?" She came down the brick walk. "Is he okay?"

"Doing great. He's looking for his dog."

"And you are?"

"Private cop. He hired me."

"Private cop? Got a license?" asked Gordon Gibbs. His breath smelled like eggs.

"I do." I pulled a card from my jacket pocket.

"Come inside, please," said Colleen.

"Colleen, no way this guy's—"

"I'm cold, Gordon. Come inside. You're being rude."

I held the card out to Gordon and followed her. When he reached for it, I let go. Forcing him to snatch, miss, and bend over for it.

Mackenzie! Get your act together! Grow up!

I enjoyed following Colleen into her home. She had

ten years on me, but she took care of herself and purchased expensive jeans, and I was human. She was naturally attractive but not overpowering. Like Jennifer Aniston, maybe. Her hair was chin length, brown dyed blond. Looked like she worked out and ate salads and got botox.

The interior of their home was boxy, the way of traditional colonials. His rounded orange bulk felt incongruous with the right angles and pompous squares of a colonial. Lots of pictures of Gordon flexing for muscle tournaments. I detected the absence of dog odor.

Ulysses's house felt like a home. This place felt hollow and staged. No money for decorating? The heat was turned down.

"What'd you say your name was?" she asked, leading me into the kitchen.

"August. Mackenzie August."

"Would you like coffee? Just made another pot."

"Thank you, no," I replied.

"And you said Ulysses is okay. I haven't heard from him recently."

"He's well. I bet text messages are a great way to communicate with him."

She turned and smiled. Genuinely. "It is. He can scroll back through and catch up."

"But he hates technology."

"So you *have* met him. My ex-husband."

"He hired me to look for his dog."

"I knew it," said Gordon behind us. He smacked his hand on the kitchen counter. "Something about that dumbass dog. Remember, Coll? I told you. Something suspicious about it."

Colleen appeared embarrassed by him. "Ulysses didn't

like dogs. And the circumstances were odd, and Gordon is suspicious and so..."

"Any idea where it is?"

"Rose told me it ran off, three years ago," said Colleen. She poured herself a cup of coffee from an expensive looking carafe. She poured me one too, just in case. "It was just a puppy. What's he want with it now?"

"I examined that stupid dog," said Gordon. "Couldn't figure it out. Nothing special on the collar. Made no sense, but I was suspicious."

"What crime do you suspect it committed?"

"What?" asked Gordon.

Colleen appeared embarrassed again.

I said, "Mind if I run through the timeline, see if I have it right?"

"Sure, anything for Ulysses."

"What?" shouted Gordon. Same word, different volume. "Why would we help that jackass?"

"He's my ex-husband, Gordon. He has amnesia. For God's sake, calm down. Go to work."

He looked at me. Might be flexing. "I own five gyms around Roanoke. Christiansburg, Blacksburg, Lynchburg, you know the drill."

"Wow. I didn't ask, but if I had I'd be impressed."

"Mr. August, you mentioned the timeline?" said Colleen. She made a shooing motion at her husband. "Go on, babe. This is upsetting you. Go to work."

"Like hell I'm leaving."

I said, "Here's what I know. You two file for divorce. It's amiable. Means friendly, Gordon. Just before the divorce finalizes, he gets a puppy. A boxer. Which everyone thinks odd because he hates dogs. Soon after, he gets into a car wreck. Rose moves in to help. She watched the dog. He comes home from the hospital with amnesia and the divorce paperwork goes through. He has visitors. And around this time the dog vanishes."

Colleen, both hands on the mug, nodded. "Sounds right. I had moved out so I don't know when the puppy disappeared."

"The trip, don't forget that fucking trip, Coll."

"What trip?" I asked.

Gordon smiled. Thrilled he knew something I didn't.

Colleen sighed. "The infamous trip. Drives Gordon crazy. Perhaps the only rash thing Ulysses ever did in his life."

"The rat bastard."

"Divorces take six months. Two months after we file, Ulysses cleans out our savings. I don't remember how much, around two million. Flies to a casino in...where, babe?"

"Monaco."

"Right. Flies to a casino in Monaco and gambles it all away."

"Son of a bitch spent all our money."

I said, "*Our* money?"

"The wife is entitled to half at the time of separation, smart guy."

"I know this, Gordon. I repeat, *our* money?"

Colleen looked embarrassed. She did that a lot. I felt bad for her.

I said, "Why didn't you sue him for the squandered money? Legally half of it was yours."

"Ulysses and I had drifted apart. Ships naturally separating with the currents, you know? I started seeing Gordon before the separation and...

"Ulysses found out."

Colleen rubbed at her forehead. "Yes. He found out. Gordon himself told him. Right before the casino trip."

"Ah hah.You felt responsible for the excursion to Monaco?"

"I did. He and I worked it out later in the form of ongoing alimony. But then the accident happened and I let it drop."

"Gordon, you idiot," I said. "Who are you really mad at? Ulysses? Or yourself?"

"What? That son of a bitch, of course."

"But if you'd waited a few weeks to brag, half of that money would now be in Colleen's bank account."

"Whatever, buddy. I own a ton of gyms. So anyway, that dog ain't here. Now take off."

"Actually, Mr. August," she said. She caught my eye and held it with meaning. "I'm about to leave. And Gordon is late. Maybe we can talk later?"

"I understand."

Gordon looked triumphant.

She grabbed her purse and we all went out the front door into the cold together. She opened the garage with the keypad and got into a little red Miata. In my Accord I backed out first. Gordon glared at me the whole way. At the first side street, I pulled off and parked. A moment later, Gordon raced by in the yellow H2. Heavens, what a racket. A moment after that, the red Miata slowly passed. Colleen saw my car, turned around, and parked behind me. She got out. I reached across to open the door, and she slid into my passenger seat.

She closed the door and there was silence and she smelled clean.

"I'm sorry about Gordon. He's...protective," she said.

"Yeah, but those pecs."

"That's what I thought. But beauty is vain, Mr. August. He owns five gyms and I help, but we don't make a lot. I'm still mad at Ulysses and Gordon in equal parts. I went from having plenty to very little. Anyway I can answer your questions better without him. And I still love Ulysses like a friend, and I want to help."

"The dog, the divorce, and the wreck. Coincidence?"

"I don't know about the dog. That still befuddles me. But the other two are not coincidence. When Ulysses crashed the car, he was blind drunk."

"Was he," I said intelligently.

"Yes. Not widely publicized. And he wasn't a drinker. Still isn't. His friends and I suspect he'd been out celebrating the divorce."

"With friends?"

"With a lover. A woman."

"Who?" I asked.

"I don't know. No one does."

"How do you know about her?"

She shifted in the car, kind of tucked a knee under. She smelled nice and she was pretty enough that I didn't risk looking at her. No need to tempt fate. Eyes straight ahead, like Batman's would be. She said, "My daughter told me. She knew about a woman, but not her identity. To be honest, Mr. August, that woman doesn't matter much to me. I hate her. Not because he took up with her, but because she left. Ulysses deserved better."

A mysterious woman was in the picture. And Ulysses had been drunk. Crucial details the man himself couldn't remember.

A fascinating case. I was stimulated.

A respectful moment passed.

"Gordon being Gordon," she continued, "he suspects

this woman convinced Ulysses to fly to the casino and spend it all, before I got half. Or, and this will truly illustrate Gordon's paranoia, that maybe Ulysses won even *more* and that somehow the dog is related. Like the dog was worth millions or the dog's collar had the combination to a bank vault, or something else wild and implausible."

A dog worth millions. An eye-opening idea. Ulysses said the dog was the key...the key to a fortune?

"Was there a collar?" I asked.

"Yes. Gordon checked. Standard collar from the store with Ulysses's phone number on it."

I made a hmmm noise. I should have something better to say. What would Kinsey Millhone ask? No idea. So I hmmm'ed.

"May I ask, why does he want the dog now? After three years? I'm surprised he remembers."

I debated telling her. She was the ex-wife, after all. In most movies, she'd be trouble. But Colleen struck me as good willed, and more than willing to hide things from her idiot husband. And, if I told the truth, maybe so would she. If she had more truths to reveal.

And maybe she would like me more.

I said, "He doesn't remember the dog. But he left notes in the journal, telling himself not to forget it. And that the dog is important."

"Important? How so?"

"I don't know. Neither does he. Maybe the dog has learned to talk and will tell us, once found."

"What does Rose think?" she asked.

"That the dog is long gone. But she thinks it'll ease some part of Ulysses's mind, once the matter is settled."

Colleen nodded absently. "She would know. Rose is a saint. I keep fearing one day she'll pack up and leave, because she's a godsend. Otherwise…I don't know. Maybe my daughter and I would help out. Imagine him there without help. It's the simple things that are hardest—have I eaten or not? Have I showered or not? Did I just get back from a jog? Some people with his condition fall to pieces, constantly eating or starving or…it's hard."

"I'm sure."

"But thank goodness for Rose."

"Would your daughter know anything about Georgina Princess Steinbeck?"

"Alex? Maybe. You could call her. She's at college, Virginia Tech. She and her father remain close."

I nodded. "I will."

She put her hand on mine and squeezed. It wasn't anything more than one human being expressing gratitude to another. "Thank you for helping him. Poor Ulysses, I hope he finds the dog. Or gets a new one, or finds peace some other way. Keep me posted?"

"Absolutely."

8

I t would be a waste of my time.

I knew it would be, no question.

But I went anyway, to Walter Lowe's office. Walter was another private detective, from whom patrons could 'Get the Lowe Down' on Roanoke.

Slimy slogans like that necessitated my potpourri.

He shared the top floor of a house, formerly a grand brick residence with wide porch, and now a commercial spot downtown. The main floor consisted of four offices, a communal bathroom, and a staircase. He shared the top floor with a guy who did taxes four months of the year and a graphic designer who needed a space out of his basement to work. Walter Lowe's office door was open and I went in.

He sat in one of his client chairs, reclined, playing on his phone. He looked like an overweight extra in a movie about twenty-year high school reunions. His shirt wasn't tucked in —I glanced down at myself and decided not to judge.

He looked up to see me and went back to his phone. "Whaddaya doin, Mack."

"Walter."

"Heard you might be gone, gone for good. I was real broken up about it."

"Where'd you hear that?"

He shrugged. "People talk. Heard a rumor you mouthed off to the wrong guy, somebody with connections."

I looked at his phone screen—he was killing zombies with his thumbs. I walked around the other side of his desk and sat. The spring sagged and the cushion had long given up the ghost. No wonder he used the client chair. He had no laptop. No bookshelves. No books. No potpourri. No music played. Two certificates on the wall, claiming membership to the National Association of Legal Investigators and the Private Investigators Association of Virginia. On his desk there was a smaller sign that stated he accepted credit cards, including Diner's Club.

What the hell was Diner's Club?

Without taking his eyes off the screen, he plucked a tissue from the box between the chairs, blew his nose, wiped it, and threw the wad into an accumulating pile near the waste basket.

"Whaddaya doing, Mack? Got a big important case? Gonna rescue the governor or something? Come to watch me in action?"

I put on my best Philip Marlowe. "It was a chilly day outside, one of those temperatures that makes a man consider hanging up his gun and moving to West Palm where the dames never wear overcoats. Cold outside but not in my office where I sweated bullets. Why? Life panic, that's why. Existential angst and loneliness, that's why. To hell with the reasons, that's why. I hadn't slept in three days, that's why, and my old pals Jim and Jack were banging inside my head. My name's Walter Lowe. I know because it says so on my door. It also says I'm a private investigator, though I can't find any other evidence to back it up. I don't even sit in my own chair. The walk's too far and I limp like a cheap hooker. Maybe I'd get lucky and a high-breasted girl from Roanoke would fall in my lap on accident and give me something to do. Until then, my only friend was my smart phone and I'd keep playing it. Because I knew how to, damn it, and a guy's got to know how to do something. I was out of cheap gin and the day was still young. Hopefully danger would walk in off the street like a Bengal tiger into a Burmese orphanage, but until then my revolver would—"

"Mack."

"Yes, Walter."

"Maybe you tell me what the hell you're doing?"

"I'm monologuing."

"You're what?" He hadn't looked up from his phone.

"This is how us private detectives think. Don't you watch the classics?"

"Like Magnum P.I.?"

"You wanna get shot, Walter?"

"Why is the girl high-breasted? Not that I'm complaining."

"Once you learn to read, go back and read Sam Spade and Mickey Spillane and Raymond Chandler. They'll explain it."

"Who?"

"Hard-boiled fiction."

"I don't get it."

"Walter!" I slammed my hand on the table, hard enough that I heard splintering. He jumped and dropped the phone. "Sit up straight! Tuck in your shirt! Stop playing video games! The hell's the *matter* with you? You're going nowhere like this!"

"Jee-zus, Mack. Scared the shit outta me." In fact he was holding his breath.

"Practice for having a teenager one day. How'd I do?"

"Made me drop my..." He fumbled for the device on the ground and grunted with exertion.

"I was your life coach, Walter, I'd inform you that you're pathetic."

"Got stuff needs doing, but I don't wanna right now. With you gone, I get more calls. A lot of witnesses to interview. You know what really sucks, Mack? They call and ask about my schedule and then they ask if I know where you went. 'Are you busy, and oh hey where's that other guy we like better than you?' I don't mind though, whatever. I tell'em you're dead."

"I got an idea."

"What's that."

"Do the jobs well. And quickly."

"You're saying I don't usually?" said Walter.

"I'm saying, do these jobs well and they'll call more often."

"Eh. We'll see. I don't like to set a high standard."

"I'm looking for Ulysses's dog. Tell me something I don't know and I'll buy your next lunch."

"Who? Why would I know that?" he said.

"Ulysses Steinbeck. You took his money about a year ago and looked for a week."

"Amnesia guy?"

"Amnesia guy."

"I didn't find out anything, Mack. How'm I supposed to locate a runaway dog from half a decade ago?"

"Would have been two years, at the time."

Walter shrugged and looked at his phone. "I was close to a new high score, Mack. I hope you feel rotten about that.

How's a guy supposed to find a runaway dog from two years ago?"

"Resourcefulness and resilience."

"I can't even spell those."

"Where'd you look for the dog?"

"I checked the local pounds."

"And..."

"Scrolled back through the social media accounts of him and his family. Saw a few photos of the puppy but nothing that helped."

"You talk to his ex-wife?" I said.

"Tried. Her new husband ran me off."

"Did he," I said. "Gordon?"

"Yeah, that's the guy. Bigger than you. You go looking for Colleen, take backup. Or a bazooka."

"What if I'm tougher than you are?"

"Don't matter. Even you, Mack, you'll back down from this freak. One of the rage monsters on steroids."

"Sounds terrifying. Anything else?"

"Don't think so. Best part of that case, amnesia guy forgot me soon as he hired me. Easy thousand bucks. His nurse what's-her-name didn't seem to care much either way."

"Her name's Rose and I'm fond of her."

"You would be."

"As I feared, Walter, you're no help."

"No lunch?"

"Not even a cracker."

"You won't find the dog. It's long gone. I couldn't find it, you won't find it. You and I, we're the same. Except you work out and take care of yourself and try hard at life. Take away all the stuff you *do*, other than that, we're twins. So where'd you go, anyway? Last couple months?"

"Italy. And a honeymoon with my wife."

"Hell, I didn't realize. Congratulations. That's exciting. I was married once." He turned the zombie game back on his screen. "It didn't work."

"Didn't it? Hard to believe."

9

Colleen suggested I call her daughter, Alex Steinbeck. I did one better—I went to see her. Much can be learned from observation of a person under stress. Not that she would be. But how would I know over the phone?

Blacksburg, Virginia might be the coldest place in the continental United States. It sits on top of mountains and the wind howls and the temperature never rises and I hated it. I parked on campus and actively expressed abhorrence.

I looked her up. She lived in Johnson Hall—upper quad, classic Virginia Tech structure, three floors of Hokie stone. I called her cell and it went to voice mail.

I texted.

Hi. I'm working with your father Ulysses and I'd like to talk, if that's okay. He gave me your number. I'll call again in thirty seconds.

I pressed send and waited.

She called me back after fifteen.

"Hi, yes, it's me, Alex—sorry, I was in a class. Is everything okay? With my dad?"

"Didn't mean to alarm you, he's fine. He hired me and I'm hoping I can ask you a few questions."

I heard lots of movement on her end. "You had me spooked. With his condition, I worry. Sure I can help, happy to."

"When can you meet?"

"I'm in Blacksburg at the moment."

Yes, I know, I'm a creepy stalker in a car outside. That felt like an unfortunate thing to admit. "Uh," I said, adroitly, to buy myself a second to think. "How about in an hour?"

"How about two? My class will be over then. You're sure there's no emergency?"

"No emergency."

"Find Owens Dining Hall, near Johnson. I'll meet you there."

As a matter of fact, I was parked next to it. And there I sat shivering for two hours. I liked what I did and Ulysses was paying me handsomely. And yet, on days when I sat freezing in a car for hours with nothing to do but listen to sports radio or podcasts on theology, a little life panic crept in. Was this what I should be doing with my life? Shouldn't I be a starting pitcher for the Washington Nationals?

At eleven I got out and hustled across the frozen tundra and into the dining hall. Just me and a thousand twenty-year olds. The girls wore leggings and leather boots, some with fur, and vests and purple gloves and scarves. All the scarves. The guys, of which there were fewer, wore sneakers or hiking boots, and jeans and khakis, and puffy Patagonia jackets. Everyone looked intelligent and trim and beautiful and socially talented.

I glanced in the mirror. I looked less so.

I recognized Alex Steinbeck by her photograph, but it didn't do her justice. In a dining hall full of pretty people, she glimmered. Picture the perfect blonde in every movie about high school or college, the one who sparkles.

"Alex," I said. "I'm Mackenzie."

"Hi Mackenzie. Gosh you're a big guy." She stamped and shivered and walked deeper into the dining hall. She was a native and I an immigrant. She pointed toward an empty table. "Sit there. I need coffee and eggs or something. Be right back."

I sat obediently.

She returned with Chick-fil-A nuggets and black coffee. She got me a coffee too, darling girl, just like her mother. She sat down and mixed in cream and Stevia.

I said, "You ever mix butter or cartilage into your coffee?"

"I do!" She sparkled again. "You do keto?"

"My roommate does. I think he's loony."

"It's a great money saver. Besides, I bet he's thin."

"Yes but beauty is vain, I heard. From your mother, actually."

"Hah. Because she married that muscular moron. He's as big as you."

"But less tough," I said.

"Think so? I mean, he lifts weight for a living."

"Strong does not equal tough."

"Nor intelligent." She sipped her coffee and ate a nugget. The kind without breading. "How can I help? Anything for my dad. He's well?"

"He's very well. Saw him recently. Sitting at his desk. He reads the newspaper, writes in his journal, goes for walks, still consults for radiologists. Doing great."

Her eyes teared and she smiled at the table. "That's Dad."

"He hired me to find his dog."

She was about to eat another nugget. And she did, after the briefest pause.

That right there. *That* was why I came. I wouldn't see the pause over a phone call.

"Georgina," said Alex.

"Right."

"The dog he had three years ago. Why does he want it back?"

She called Georgina an *it*. Like my father would. Like probably I did some.

"He doesn't know. You know him, the 'why' can be foggy. He's leaving himself notes to find it, and believes the dog is important."

"Sorry, this is weird. But...do you have proof you're actually working for him?"

I sipped my coffee. "What do you mean."

"How do I know you're trustworthy?"

"I could show you the image my bank sent me of the check he wrote. I could tell you that we sat across from each other in his office, and he wrote in three different leather journals, spending most of the time in *What is Happening Right Now*. And that in his *Who is Who* journal, I'm listed as trustworthy and reliable. You could call your mother, who should vouch for me. She told me more about the wreck than he remembers."

"She did? What'd she say?"

"That Ulysses had been drunk, which was odd because he didn't drink. And that she suspects he'd been with a woman."

Her eyes narrowed. "Did she say who?"

"She doesn't know who."

Some of the iron left her spine and her shoulders

dropped. "Sorry, Mackenzie. I should trust you, I realize. It's...it's complicated, I guess."

"How so?"

"Our family is...I don't know. Family is hard and so is our past. And Gordon thought they should get the dog in the divorce, so..."

"You wondered if I might be working for Gordon."

Half smile. "It occurred to me. But you're not."

"I'm not."

She waved at some friends walking by.

She said, "Tell me again, why does Dad want the dog? Or, let me rephrase. Do his journals give him a reason to find the dog?"

"The initial note, which was written a long time ago, reminded him not to forget the dog. The dog is the key."

"The key? As in, the dog is vital? Or the key to unlocking something?"

I shrugged. "I don't know. Rose thinks settling the matter will bring him peace, even if he won't remember details."

"Sweet Rose." Her eyes teared again. "We'd be lost without her."

"Can you tell me anything about the dog I don't know."

She leaned her cheek on her palm, elbow propped on the table. She still wore a black heavy down jacket with hood, and with her free hand she unzipped it. A sigh. "Yes. I can."

Ah hah! Clues inbound.

"I'm all ears."

"Ugh. This is going to make me look awful."

"I doubt that is possible."

Another half smile, but genuine. Like her mother. "Thanks. Okay, Mackenzie, I'll tell you. When he bought the dog, it was weird. You know? He didn't tell me why. I was in my senior year. But he did his best to keep it a secret from my mom. Then, one day, he told me the dog was mine."

"He bought Georgina for you?"

"Yes. Or he told me he did. He said I should keep it and not to give it away, especially not to my mother or Gordon. Gordon was in the picture at that point."

"So the dog was a secret and it was important, sounds like."

"Exactly. Not like a normal father/daughter gift; he thought it was somehow totemic. I was still living at home when the accident happened, but..." She winced, like the memory was painful. "I grew up wanting a dog. All my life. But I was never allowed to have one, and then......I don't know, suddenly in my senior year I didn't see the point. Nor did I have any time to train it. Isn't that awful? He gives me a gift, it's obviously important to him, and I didn't care."

"That's not awful."

She waved some more to passersby. She was popular. Me, less so. "So the accident, the hospital, the recovery. He comes home. My mom and Gordon come to visit, and Gordon is obsessed with the dog. He thinks it has something to do with money."

"The trip to the casino?" I asked.

"Right. Wow, so you know a few of our sordid secrets. I don't believe that's in the public realm. Gordon was so outraged by that trip that he got a lawyer involved. He suspected Ulysses faked the trip and hid the money somewhere, or bought the world's most expensive dog. But my father quickly produced his passport and the airline ticket to Monaco and the cashier receipts for large, *large* sums of money. Paperwork for currency exchanges, things like that. He has the documents to prove he went to Monaco and gambled. Even took a few selfies there. To force Gordon and my mom to back down, Dad agreed to pay alimony."

"You think he went to Monaco and blew the money because he hated Gordon?"

"Maybe." She nodded. "They loathe one another. Or did, I don't know if my father still remembers him. It sucks because he has less money now. I don't want to strain his finances further so I'm putting myself through school."

"Very admirable."

"Being broke rarely feels admirable."

"Better than massive debt."

"I got us off track. Sorry."

"Did the dog run away?"

"No." She looked embarrassed. Like her mother. "Gordon kept bothering the animal, so I took it to my boyfriend's house. Didn't tell anyone."

"Good idea."

She brightened. "Was it?"

"I think so. And I'm really smart."

She laughed.

I asked, "Does your boyfriend still have it?"

"No. We broke up my freshman year and he demanded I take it back. But I was in a college dorm and I'm gone all the time, flying everywhere, what am I supposed to do with a dog?"

"You fly everywhere?"

She looked embarrassed again. "Yeah, still do."

"For what?"

She held up a finger. Pulled her phone out. Pressed the screen a few times and slid the device across the table. She'd opened her Instagram account. All the photos were of her. On a beach in a bikini. In the snow in a bikini. In the water, laughing, wearing jeans and a sweater. Smiling in the wind wearing a sweater. Smiling in the rain in a bikini. Professional quality. About half the photos were watermarked with name brands.

"You're a model," I noted and slid the phone back.

"I am. Lots of girls are these days, with photoshop and selfies. I happen to get paid a little. Did you see how many followers I have?"

"Over a hundred thousand."

"Not much, to be honest, in my profession. All my classes are on Tuesdays and Thursdays, and I'm often gone Friday through Monday."

"But you're not rich?"

She laughed. A wry sound, no humor. "No. I'm broke. Instagram famous isn't really famous. It pays for school and a little extra. But," she said and she held up her thumb and fingers to make a circle shape, "zero social life. Haven't been on a date in months."

"There's no way you could take care of a dog. And you broke up with your boyfriend."

"Right." Her cheeks reddened. "So I gave Georgina away."

Ah hah. Getting closer.

"To whom?"

"A nice family on Craigslist. I forget their names."

"You still have the emails? Could I get their contact info?"

"Of course." Her posture straightened and she dazzled with pleasure. I got the feeling her sparkling and dazzling were tricks she learned to make a camera happy. "Probably still have it on my phone."

"Alex, you saint."

She smiled and squeezed my hand. Not romantic, I

thought; just one human acting friendly to another. Like mother, like daughter. "My full name is Alexandra."

"Alexandra Steinbeck. With that name, you're destined to go places, kid."

"Thanks." Another genuine smile. She scanned her screen, searching emails.

"While you look, one more question."

"Sure, Mackenzie."

"The night of the accident, Ulysses was with a woman. So your mother tells me. Who was it?"

Alex lowered the phone. Stopped searching. But she didn't look at me.

"That was an awful night."

"I'm sure."

"And, if it's okay, I don't want to discuss it. I'd rather not remember or talk about it ever again. One of those family ordeals that should stay buried." She didn't wait for a response and she resumed searching through her phone.

I was stimulated.

10

***

Back in the car, freezing, near death, I emailed the nice couple from my phone.

DEAR COHEN FAMILY,

A few years ago you adopted a boxer named Georgina Princess Steinbeck from a girl named Alex. Alex is the daughter of Ulysses, the original owner of the dog. For reasons of sentimentality, Ulysses is hoping to be reunited with Georgina and become her owner again. Do you still have Georgina? If so, would you be willing to part with her?

Sincerely,

Mackenzie

THE DRIVE HOME lasted an hour and I debated whether Alex Steinbeck and her mother Colleen Gibbs made all guys feel special and good about themselves, or if they only sparkled and smiled genuinely at me.

Probably just me, I decided.

I also wondered if this was a trick a lot of women did to build connections and trust, the physical touch thing.

I got home and checked my phone.

MACKENZIE,

We still have Georgina!! She's a great dog. We love her and don't plan to give her away. Please tell her original owner that we're sorry, and we hope he finds another dog to love!!!

Sincerely,

Ramona Cohen.

RATS.

11

M arcus Morgan met Ronnie and me for lunch at Martin's the next day. He and the owner had some arrangement where he could use the place day or night, open or closed. Perhaps they were in cahoots or perhaps they weren't in cahoots and they were just friends. Either way, we got a big table by ourselves at a window and a server dedicated solely to us who knew to be attentive while keeping her distance.

Crime definitely paid.

Marcus looked as he always did—eternally wise and stoic. Black puffer jacket by Moncler, probably worth a grand. Black slacks. Silver belt buckle and Tag Heuer watch and wedding band. His socks were black and so were the Prada loafers. He kept the jacket zipped, almost to his chin.

Each of us, because we were classy gangsters, ordered tea. I sipped mine with lemon, feeling a little goofy. My hand was too big for the cup. Ronnie sipped hers, looking like a duchess.

"So," said Marcus. He lowered his tea to the saucer. "You want out."

"Of the marijuana business," Ronnie said.

He made a grunting noise.

I said, "It can be done."

"Can be done." He nodded. "Don't happen much. Don't know how it'll work. Summers here, sweetheart that she is, got more...ah, history with the District Kings than most."

"Because I was coerced into being their actual sweetheart for a long time."

He nodded more. Slowly. "Some of them keep expecting you to show up. Got plans to carry you away, marry you on some private island and live there forever."

"That sounds nice. Who plans that?" she said.

I frowned. I didn't have a private island.

She poked me. "Teasing. Bad joke."

"Don't matter how rich they get. A foolish man is a foolish man," said Marcus. "Especially about fine ass women."

"Guilty," I said.

"Was talking about other foolish men."

"Still."

"At least you're a foolish man whose fine ass woman is foolish about you in return," said Ronnie.

Our server brought another pot of tea, set it on the table, and retreated.

"About the marijuana," I said. "None of this is legal. Is there even a precedent for selling resources such as hers?"

"Sho nuff. It happens. Underworld recognizes ownership."

"Honor among thieves."

He nodded.

"Selling, however, won't be Ronnie's panacea. Selling doesn't erase relationships," I said.

"Righto."

"There's no relational bond on my end," she said. "But on the other side, sometimes there's an anchor."

"Meaning, it's hard for you to get free from them," I said. "Because even if you think you're free, there's a rich and powerful and foolish man holding tight to the other end."

"And on some level, in their mind, they have ownership over me."

"Look at us," said Marcus with a grin. "Talking about levels of ownership, none of it legal, all of it intellectual and emotional. We deep as hell."

I said, "Do the foolish men know you were coerced into it by Darren?"

She and Marcus both nodded.

I said, "Doesn't make a difference."

She and Marcus both shook their head.

"Being honest," said Marcus. "Surprised Darren's still alive."

"He called off the contract on my life. I sent him a message, explaining that bought him sixty days."

"Sixty days to what?"

"To vanish. After sixty, I extirpate him."

"That mean kill?"

"Destroy completely."

Marcus nodded. Absently squeezed his lemon into the cup. "Cause he prostituted your girl and put two separate contracts on your head."

"Either of those be enough, if you ask me," I said.

Ronnie remained quiet.

"Gonna be a war," said Marcus. "You try."

"I know. He's hoping the threat of that will deter me."

"Will it?"

"I cannot be deterred. Some might say, I'm determined."

"How long's he got left?"

"Three weeks."

"Shit."

The way Marcus said it, sounded like, *Shee-yit.*

Ronnie said, "I'd rather you not die."

I snorted. "Die."

"So you won't?"

I snorted again. "Probably not."

"First things first," she said. "Marcus, find me a buyer. Can you do that?"

"Think maybe I buy you out myself," he said.

She smiled. Marcus and I sat up straighter; her smile made one remember one's self. She said, "I was hoping you might."

"Consolidating power and whatnot. I'm a business man first. What I think we should do? Meet with a guy. Guy on the King's board of directors, so to speak. Get his permission and have him set the price. Since we're friends and all, let a third party handle the shit."

"Get his permission?" I said. "We just shot our way out of Italy and burned the place down. Permission? I scoff at permission."

"We bad asses," he said.

"Heavens yes."

"But still. Easier this way. Fewer complications, no potential backlash."

"And hopefully," said Ronnie and she paused. Poured a little more cream into her tea and stirred it with the spoon, making soft clinking noises. She was deep in thought during the interlude and I enjoyed watching it. She made a tsk'ing noise with her teeth and continued, "No, not hopefully. I'll force them to see reason. I want out of the game, entirely. This could be the final point of separation."

"Thought you wanted to revamp the way Kings treat the whores," said Marcus.

"I do." She shrugged, a motion I always found charming. "Prostitution isn't going away. In fact it's becoming more prevalent, I read, with our society thumbing its nose at marriage. And no one takes care of the girls. But it's a problem bigger than me and so I'll start simple. Here in Roanoke. And then perhaps enlarge my territory."

"You know the Kings consider Roanoke their territory."

She said, "We can coexist."

"Kings don't like coexisting."

"I'll make them. In fact, I'm looking forward to the meeting. A few things I need to get straight with your bosses."

"Egads," I said.

12

I met with Courtney Farmer at Scrambled, my favorite breakfast eatery. Courtney was a local veterinarian, recommended by Stackhouse. She was tall and trim, straight shoulder-length brown hair dyed blonde. The elegant structure of her face was prominent, indicating she was a jogger, and her eyes were wide, as though in constant astonishment. She had the posture of a cotillion patron. Underneath her jacket she wore a white shirt monogrammed with Roanoke Animal Hospital.

She held up her mimosa and said, "I like to let the day know who's boss, right from the start."

I lofted my coffee in return, ashamed at having no didactic reason for it.

Our breakfast came—we both got their famous scrambled eggs.

I said, "I hear you're an expert on dogs."

"Expert is pushing it. I like them, obviously. I own two. What kind do you have?"

"I don't."

Her eyes widened farther and her posture, which was good, became even more erect. "You lie."

"Never had one."

"What a monster. You must not have a soul."

"You dog owners feel strongly about this."

"But you're in the market to adopt one?"

"Adopt? What fascinating jargon. One *adopts* a dog? Does one adopt a couch? Or pillow? Or pair of sneakers?"

She drank some mimosa and watched me without comment. She looked playful, but she also looked as though wondering if I was a serial killer. With good cheekbones.

I cleared my throat. "Let me start over and try to be less heinous. I've been hired to find a dog and I'm chasing a lead."

"The dog ran away?"

"No, I found it, actually. It's a tangential lead."

She ate some eggs. Said, "I didn't know private detectives did things like this. You're a professional mystery solver?"

"I like that. Might get it on my card."

"What tangential lead about a dog you already found can I help with? You're paying for breakfast, after all."

"The dog is important to my client. But he has amnesia and he can't remember why."

Courtney gave a half snort, which sounded both derisive and ladylike. "You don't need a reason for a dog to be important. A dog is important, end of story."

"This one more so."

"In what way?"

"That's what I'm chasing down."

"Is your client Doctor Ulysses Steinbeck?" she asked with a suspicious squint and half smile.

"That's confidential."

"He *is*."

"That's confidential and yes he is. You know him?"

"Of course I know him. We go back fifteen years. But Ulysses would never have a dog. He's soulless, like you."

"In fact he did. For a week or two, before the crash."

She made a, "Huhm," noise of surprise. Finished her mimosa. Set it down, picked up her water glass. "I'm shocked. The poor man. Now he wants the dog back?"

"Yes. But he doesn't know why."

"Fascinating."

"Isn't it. Here's my question. How much could it possibly be worth?"

She arched an eyebrow. "It?"

"Sorry. She. How much could *she* possibly be worth?"

"Dogs are priceless."

I groaned. "Let me rephrase. Is it possible he spent a million dollars on the dog?"

She sat up straighter, choking a little on the water. She set the glass down, wiped her mouth, and laughed. "Maybe. Can the dog fly?"

"No. But I'm wondering if he bought the offspring of a Westminster winner, or something similar."

"Even then he'd only pay ten thousand, maybe. Why would you think he'd pay a million for a puppy?"

"Because dogs are priceless, you succubus."

She laughed again. Dabbed at her eyes and picked up her fork. "Unless the dog came with a trust fund of $950,000, I cannot imagine anyone paying that much. Not even hoity-toity dog handlers."

"Rats."

"Clearly there's more to your case than meets the eye."

"Clearly."

Courtney's leg was crossed and she kicked it a little. "You'll crack the case. Elementary, my dear Watson."

"Hey. I handle the cheesy quotes around here."

"Give me your card. I'm friends with oodles of lawyers and you look big and strong enough to do their dirty work."

I took out my card. "Strength is not the issue. It's brainpower."

"Then you're lucky you're pretty."

"That's just the mimosa talking," I said.

No it wasn't; I'm pretty.

13

Rose Bridges met me at the door. She was barefoot again, despite the chill, and wore a cabled wool pullover sweater. She waved me in and asked if I wanted tea.

I declined.

"Go on in, Mr. August. He's having a good day."

"What are bad days like?"

"Nothing terrible. He gets more frustrated than usual with his condition. More antsy."

"Thank you, Rose."

"Call if you need me."

Steinbeck sat at his desk, reading the newspaper. Another turtleneck. Corduroy pants and he wore leather loafers. He glanced at me over the bifocals.

I knocked on the door frame. "Dr. Steinbeck."

He automatically glanced at the whiteboard over the bifocals—no, I wasn't expected. He folded the newspaper crisply and set it aside. Capped the pen he'd been using to mark it. "Please. Come in."

"My name is—"

He held up a finger. Smiled and thought a moment. "I

remember your scent. We met before. The olfactory part of my brain was not damaged."

I nodded.

"One moment." He pulled his *Who is Who* journal close. Paused. Instead he opened *What is Happening Now* and flipped to today. Ran his fingertip down the edge, murmuring to himself. Turned back to yesterday. Repeated the process. Softly he said, "One moment, please." He glanced at me, looking for clues, and took another breath through his nose. Flipped back another day. He made a "Hmmm," noise and paused. Tapped the page with his finger. "You're Mackenzie August."

"I am."

"You're helping find the dog. This is our first meeting since the initial encounter."

"Powerful nose you have."

"Olfactory stimuli are handled in the parietal lobe, a part of my brain which functions fully. Anterograde amnesia is caused by trauma to the temporal cortex."

"Caused by trauma *and* sometimes by intoxication. I looked it up."

"Yes but I don't drink. So." He shrugged.

Ah hah! A clue.

His ex-wife Colleen Gibbs and his daughter Alex Steinbeck both agreed he didn't drink. Yet Colleen said he was blind drunk the night of the crash. Rose said he drove his car straight off a cliff, no other vehicles involved.

So someone was lying or someone forgot the facts. Or both. But why? Could the obvious answer be the truth, that he was merely lurching through emotional distress because of the divorce and his wife seeing a new man? That he'd *adopted* a wounded boxer puppy as a way of saving himself?

I said, "I found Georgina Princess Steinbeck. It's...excuse me, *she's* in the care of a nice family living nearby."

He released a long breath of air like he'd been holding it. Leaned forward, retrieved the fountain pen, and wrote on the page. "Perfect. Have you seen the dog yet?"

"No. Just verified through email."

"Okay. Good, good." He finished writing, dropped the pen, and drummed his fingers on the table. Glanced at his journals out of habit. "We should buy it from them, I suppose."

"I already offered. They aren't interested. For some people, dogs are priceless."

Crazy people, but people none the less.

"Everyone has a price."

"How high are you willing to go?"

"I don't know. We'll consult with Rose," he said. "I wake up every day without a clue how much is in any bank account. To be honest, it's a nice way to live. But I think I'd like to get the dog and money is no object."

"Spend and spare not?"

"Something like that," he said.

"Have you decided what you'll do once you have the dog?"

"I..." He blinked. "No. I don't want to *own* the dog."

"Then what happens when I drop her on your doorstep?"

"No, no, don't do that."

"I am bamboozled, Ulysses."

He scrubbed a hand through his perfect brown hair. For a flicker in time, my body registered the unimaginable frustration he must feel on a daily basis. He said, "Me too, I'm afraid. In my mind, the getting is more important than the having. I want to get the dog, but not possess it. Does that make sense? No, I know it doesn't."

"Tell me about the car crash."

That surprised him. "Why? Is that germane?"

"I don't know. Before the divorce you did a series of uncharacteristic things. You got a dog. You gambled away your life savings. You got drunk."

"I did? I don't remember gambling. Or getting drunk."

"That's the rumor."

He shook his head. "I doubt it. You'll need proof to convince me."

There *was* proof, apparently, somewhere, about the gambling trip. But that would serve no purpose.

"You don't remember the casino trip?"

"The casino trip," he said slowly. "The casino trip. I haven't thought about that in...I remember it like an old old movie. There are no details but...when I focus on it, I lose it in the fog."

I said, "Could the dog be worth a fortune?"

"I don't see how."

"Were you dating anyone immediately before the divorce finalized?"

"I was not," he said. With a wince.

"Are you positive?"

"No romance, not that I remember." He shifted in his chair, crossed his legs the other way, and fidgeted. As though suddenly anxious. There was another woman, according to my sources. Did his body remember but his brain forget?

I said, "Trying to access these memories causes you distress."

"Yes, well phrased. I..." He closed his eyes and shifted again. "Sudden dread so powerful it hurts physically. But I cannot identify the source."

"If we knew what happened during that period of your life, we might discover the *why*. As in, *why* is the dog important."

"There was a car crash. That's all I know. Perhaps the full story is somewhere in my notes. I'd rather not delve."

"You still want to buy the dog," I said.

"Yes."

"Because it's the key to something."

He nodded. "Exactly."

"But you don't know to what. And you don't want to think about it too hard. And you don't want to keep the animal. You're like a dog chasing your tail except you don't have one and you can't stop."

"Right." He took off the bifocals and dropped them onto the desk with a clatter. "Mr. August, this is ludicrous. I know it is. You don't need to tell me. I am ashamed and frustrated with myself. Would you please find out *why* the dog is important? And please keep the dog at your home?"

I sat up a little straighter, the way I'd seen Dr. Courtney Farmer do. "*My* home."

"Please."

"I can't. I have a kid. And a Manny. And a father who doesn't love dogs."

"Please, Mr. August. Name your price."

"It's not about the money. It's about the..."

"Yes?" he asked.

"My lackadaisicalness, primarily."

"Children love dogs, right?"

"I wouldn't know. They do in the movies. But let's circle back to that in a minute. I can find out to what the dog is the key. Probably. Be easier with your notes."

He laid his hand protectively across the leather journals. His memories. To my surprise, the handsome man issued a tear. Spilled down under his chin, as it ought. "I understand. But only as a last resort. It will be laying my life open to an unbearable extent."

"I understand. I'll try without."

He pressed a button on the underside of his desk and within the house a chime sounded. He wiped his eyes and soon Rose came.

Ulysses smiled at her appearance. As do daffodils in Spring. "Rose, we need to write this man a check. How much can I afford?"

"That's a good question, Dr. Steinbeck." She tapped the white board against the wall, the one placed where he could see it always. She spoke like a nurse who had to be firm with her patient. But a kind nurse. "Three hospitals sent pictures for your opinion. Are you going to keep working?"

"Ah. Yes. I must've forgot. I'll do that immediately. But we're not broke?"

She smiled. "No, we're getting by. Read those pictures and you'll have enough to send a little to Alex."

"Excellent. Pay Mr. August for another week of work, please, and make it out extra for..." He looked at me for clues. "How much will it take to buy the dog from...from... whoever has it? Ten thousand?"

"Plenty. I'll bring you change."

"Who has it? I forgot."

"Nice couple on Craigslist." I did not mention her name was Ramona Cohen and that Ramona used far too many exclamation points in her emails.

He picked up his pen and began scratching.

I said, "About Georgina—"

"You'll keep it at your place?" he said.

I made a deeply puerile and lugubrious noise.

"Did you hear that?" I said. "That was a deeply puerile and lugubrious sigh."

"You don't want for vocabulary, Mr. August. But I am desperate."

I made the noise again. "I'm willing to either keep it at my place or find a secondary location just as good and just as accessible and just as safe. That's the only deal I'll make."

He looked up. Smiled with relief. "I accept."

14

Ramona Cohen, the nice lady from Craigslist, and Ronald, her nice husband, lived in Botetourt on five acres of land. Their home was a cheap imitation of a ranch farmhouse, sided with yellow vinyl, trimmed with white vinyl, built to code and not a nail farther. But one did not purchase this property for the house; one purchased it for the vista. Built on a hill looking west, the acre below their front porch was cleared of trees. I came up the long gravel drive, parked, and admired the view of Mill Mountain, maybe ten miles distant. Roanoke Valley—such a beautiful place no wonder Lewis and Clark named it the Star City of the South

They did not name it that. Someone else did. But they should've.

Ramona opened her front door and three large dogs spewed forth, howling. To my untrained eye, these were the largest dogs ever spawned. I coolly got back into my car and closed the door.

I didn't know a lot about dogs but I knew these weren't

boxers. More like a wolf mated with a bear. And then a horse.

Ramona, the rascal, laughed and shouted. Her voice sounded muffled. "Don't worry, they don't bite! Just being friendly!"

I did not budge. I didn't get this handsome by wrestling with hounds from hell.

"Rex! Comet! Zeus! Get back here!" she shouted.

After a moment of delirious slobbering on my driver side window, the wild and rabid curs retreated to the house.

"Well, come on!" called Ramona, waving at me. "It's cold!"

Rather not, Ramona.

But I did, issuing a series of puerile and lugubrious noises. With infinite regret I followed her inside and she closed the door behind me.

That. *That* right there was why my father didn't let me have a dog as a child—dog hair everywhere, thick nests of it in the corners. And the heavy animal musk.

Thankfully no massive animal bit off my foot. The barking sounds came from the back of the house now, behind a closed door. Ramona watched me, chuckling at my fear and stupidity. Her husband came down the hall. Said, "God almighty, what a racket. Never need an alarm system, though."

By his side, eager and alert and handsome, walked a boxer. Had to be Georgina Princess. She came up to his knees. Big dark eyes, light brown coat, a powerful white chest, ears tuned forward. This animal, unlike the others, maintained some self respect. She inspected me with interest, like, *So you're the wimp.*

If dogs can smile, she did.

I stuck my hand out. "Mackenzie August, thanks for humoring my visit."

Ronald shook it. "Well, I'm Ron and this here's Ramona. Not sure what good it'll do you."

"This is Georgina?" I asked.

The dog came forward and placed her paw into my hand.

Well.

How about that. I was charmed.

"Yes, we call her Georgie," said Ramona. "She's the sweetest dog, I love her to pieces."

"I can see why. I know nothing about dogs, but she strikes me as the best one."

Ronald chuckled.

Ramona laughed. "We like her."

"I hear her original owner wants her back," said Ronald. "But you ain't him."

"Correct," I said. I released Georgina's paw and scratched her behind the ears.

"After some odd three years? Ain't that strange."

"It is a little strange, Ronald. I admit it. But so are the circumstances surrounding the request."

Ramona grabbed my jacket and pulled me into the kitchen. A farmhouse kitchen with a red tea kettle, decorative plates displayed above the cabinets, doilies at each chair at the table, and oil paintings of dogs with dead birds clenched in their maws.

She said, "You want coffee?"

"Thank you, no. Still have a steaming mug in the car."

"So what're the strange circumstances?" asked Ronald. Looked like a farmer gone to retirement, maybe sixty, built lean but sturdy. A no-nonsense face, though open and friendly. He lowered to a wooden kitchen chair with a grunt.

"Georgina was *adopted* by a guy in Roanoke, three years ago," I said. The animal in question followed me to the kitchen island and politely waited to be scratched some more. I acquiesced. "But a week or two after the adoption, he was involved in a serious car wreck. Hospitalized and came away with amnesia. He couldn't care for the dog and neither could his daughter, so they gave Georgina away on Craigslist. To you wonderful folk."

Each time she heard her name, Georgina's ears perked.

"Oh my," said Ramona. She placed her hand on her chest. "Amnesia? Really, like in the movies?"

"Usually in the movies the person cannot remember their past. This is a little different in that he cannot create new memories."

Ronald said, "And he wants the dog back?"

"That's the short version." I nodded.

"Why?"

"He doesn't know. He barely remembers Georgina, but he wakes up every day with the vague notion something's missing. And he leaves himself notes about her."

"Notes?" asked Ramona.

"That's what he has instead of short-term memory. Notes and journals."

"How about that. You're right, strange circumstances."

"Why didn't Georgina attack my car, like the other dogs?" I asked.

Ramona beamed like a proud parent. "Cause she's too much of a princess. She really grew into her name. Look at her, just a'sitting there."

"Old Georgie is a peculiar dog." Ronald sniffed, but with approval. "Most boxers are overly active, you ask me. Maybe too friendly. But not her. Don't bark, don't beg, don't jump on people. Don't even like the pack much."

I asked, "She's aggressive with the others?"

"No, no, didn't say that. I just mean, she don't participate in the lunacy. Like you saw. Plays outside with them some, but prefers people."

"I'm the same way."

"I could tell, the way you hid in your car!" Ramona cackled, the heartless wench.

"I wasn't hiding. I was evaluating."

"Hah!"

"Have you ever noticed anything unusual about her? Other than her pleasant temperament?" My unspoken question—something that would make her worth a million dollars? Or two?

"Like what?" Ronald worried at his ear.

"I don't know. I'm not overly familiar with dogs. Did she have any injuries or scars?"

"No, nothing like that," said Ramona. "I'd have noticed."

"How many dogs do you have total?"

"Six," said Ramona. "The four you seen plus two more in the basement."

"Too damn many, you ask me."

"It's your lucky day, Ronald," I said. "I've been sent with a checkbook to reduce your burden by one."

Ronald grunted. "Mighty strange request."

"I know. Even for a mercenary like me, it borders on heartless," I said.

"Another dog won't do?"

"Apparently not. The puppy just outside his memory haunts him," I said. Admitting Ulysses didn't actually like dogs would reduce my bargaining power.

Ramona sat next to her husband. Squeezed her hands between her knees and considered crying. "But I love her."

"You heard Mr. August, the man's got amnesia. 'Sides, we

got five others. Still too many. You said it yourself, not a week ago."

Georgina Princess Steinbeck watched Ramona with interest. I kept up the scratching. Her mouth opened and she panted with pleasure.

Georgina, not Ramona.

I said, "I can pay you enough to buy two replacements. Pure bred boxer puppies."

"God almighty, we don't want *more*. And not puppies, no thank you," said Ronald.

"Mr. August, it's not about the money," she said.

"I know it's not. And I don't mean to insult you."

"But the money would help." Ronald winked. "Few things round here need replacing, anyways."

Ramona blinked away some tears. "My husband needs replacing, maybe."

I grinned.

THIRTY MINUTES later I loaded a flattened metal crate into my trunk while Ramona watched and cried from the porch. Ronald put his arm around her and waved—I paid them handsomely. Let it never be said Mackenzie August isn't generous with other people's money.

Georgina leaped gracefully into the passenger seat when I beckoned.

"Good girl," I said.

She watched the farmhouse fade into the distance as we bounced down the gravel drive, and she started to whine.

A lugubrious sound.

15

G eorgina had never met a toddler.
Kix had never interacted with a dog that I could remember.

They watched each other the way Neil Armstrong might've, had he and an alien encountered one another on the moon—emotions indescribable, though enthusiasm and disbelief were near the top. Georgina ran around the main level of Chez August, smelling the smells, but returned inexorably to Kix. She thought he was a riot, this person smaller than herself.

I stayed near in case she decided to lick his face or bite his head. Who knew what these wild animals were capable of. I also stayed near in case Kix tried to rip Georgina's ear off.

After thirty minutes of observation I decided Georgina understood on some subterranean level that this human required extra care; she volitionally eased off the gas near Kix.

Kix wobbled on his feet, screaming with pleasure the whole time.

That evening, for twenty minutes straight as I mixed a large taco salad, the dog ran up the rear staircase and came down the front. Over and over, looking more pleased with each revolution.

Kix laughed from his chair.

Watch this, father, she's going to do it again. What a dumb animal! I'm so happy.

"Dog," I said. "Kix, say dog."

"Dog," said Kix.

"Very good. Dog."

"Dog."

I picked up a tennis ball Ramona had sent and I rolled it across the room. Georgina chased it and I said, "Fetch."

Kix laughed.

"Fetch. Kix, say fetch."

"Fish."

Georgina came back, pleased. I told her she was a good dog, and I took the ball and rolled it again. "Fetch."

"Fish," said Kix.

"Fetch. Rhymes with...ah...homestretch."

This is a stupid game, Father, and I hate it.

"Fetch."

"Fish."

Our crew returned home at intervals and rattled the door, and she growled until I told her to cool it. Then, intruder personally vouched for, she welcomed them with fervor.

Manny and Ronnie successively lost any shred of dignity and got down on all fours, wild animals themselves. Lost in the throes of joy, Georgina leaped *over* Manny.

Sheriff Stackhouse told her she was a good dog and scratched her behind the ears.

Timothy August smiled benevolently. "You found her, then. Short hair, at least. And no oppressive odor."

Kingdom of God, up in here.

As we ate, Georgina sat erect nearby, watching us and watching the door. Expecting Ramona to walk through any second.

That evening, Manny, Ronnie and I took our ease on the leather couch watching a cooking show. Ronnie's head rested on my shoulder, a glass of wine perched within her fingers. Georgina was curled near a heating vent in the floor. Eyes on the front door.

"Will you keep her here?" asked Ronnie.

"I think I have to. She put her paw into my hand, for goodness sake."

"Where will she sleep?"

"The floor?"

"Yes, but where?"

"No idea," I said.

"What did you feed her?"

"Umm."

Ronnie raised from my shoulder. "You haven't fed her?"

"No. Dogs eat, I guess, huh."

Manny snorted and stood. "I'll cut her some chicken. Maybe she wants beer?"

"No. What? No," said Ronnie. "What is *wrong* with you two?"

"We fed dogs beer in Puerto Rico, mamita. They liked it."

"Chicken is a good idea, Manuel, and a dish of water," she said.

"Ay. Probably right. Dog's worth two million dollars or something?"

I said, "Don't think so. Georgina's involved somehow in the whole Steinbeck farrago but I don't believe she herself is worth more than any other dog. The family secrets are still hidden."

"And Ulysses wants you to uncover them."

"Yes. His subconscious wants me to, though he verbalized it with different words."

From the kitchen Manny asked, "What secrets?"

"I don't know yet. His ex-wife's new husband suspects chicanery and he might be right. The daughter has awful memories of something but she won't spill. There was a woman involved he can't remember. He didn't drink, but he got blind drunk that night. He went gambling—very uncharacteristic of him. And the dog. It all adds up to something. But neither of us knows what. He refuses to dig into it, which is why he hired me."

"How will you?" asked Ronnie. Her breath was on my neck, her free hand around my bicep.

"Successive approximation."

She undid the top two buttons of my shirt. Reached around to the back and tugged on my collar to expose my neck and the upper part of my back. She traced the lines of the world's most humiliating tattoo, given to me in Italy.

"King," she said sleepily. "Fits you. You're good at your job."

"You're good at yours. Doesn't mean you should be branded with it."

She snickered. "You're a King."

"A king who can never take my shirt off in public."

"I agree, but only because I'd be jealous of all the girls checking out your pecs."

Manny snorted again. "Pecs." Georgina detected food preparation and she waited by his side with courteous expectancy. He lowered a bowl of cubed chicken and bowl of water, and Georgina practically inhaled both.

"Dios mio, she was hungry," he muttered and cleaned up the kitchen floor.

Ronnie yawned. "Marcus called. We're having dinner soon with his friend from Washington. I don't know him. Your attendance is expected."

I said, "To talk about the sale of your property."

"Yes."

Manny came back and sat in the overstuffed reading chair. "I should be there too?"

"No thank you, Manuel. This is a safe and civilized meeting."

Manny jerked a thumb at himself. "I'm civilized as heck."

"What she means is, we don't need you to come kill anyone or prevent us from being killed."

"Sounds like a boring dinner. Gonna knit too?"

"I hope it's boring. But these things usually aren't," said Ronnie.

"Big Mack, when are we gonna talk with Darren What's-his-face? Need to get things off my chest with that *pendejo*."

"He's got a few more weeks to vanish. But he won't. And then we go," I said.

"What if he decides to take you out first?"

"Marcus has his pulse on the situation. He'll alert us."

"What if Darren decides to do something about Marcus?"

I nodded. "A possibility. Lines are being drawn. The situation is fluid."

"You and your honor, *migo*. Gonna get all three of us killed."

"Abandon your body but never your honor."

"Who you quoting?"

"Someone stupendous, no doubt."

"If you die, I call dibs on Ronnie."

She smiled. "Deal."

I said, "If I die, throw her into the coffin with me. She won't mind."

"Mackenzie."

"Yes Ronnie."

"I'm tired of sleeping at my place. And I'm drowsy. May I sleep here tonight?"

"Mi casa es su casa," I said.

"I can translate, you need me to," said Manny.

She stood and stretched. Worth the price of admission. "I'm going to bed. You can wake me up later, if you like, for purposes of recreation."

"Deal," said Manny.

"Not you. Wait until I die," I said.

~

AT THREE IN THE MORNING, a gorgeous and needy girl prodded me until I sat up, blinking and stupid.

Georgina Princess's paws rested on my bed and she whined softly at a decibel near the upper limit of my range. She'd been poking my arm with her cold nose.

I rubbed my eyes and whispered. "Yes?"

I am lonely.

"Do you need to go out? Nature calls?"

No I am lonely and I do not know this place well and it does not smell like me and there are no other dogs.

I slipped out of bed, careful not to wake sleeping beauty. Shoved feet into slippers—they were red and black checkered, very manly, which made it okay—and walked Georgina Princess down the stairs to the back door. I opened it. She sat down and looked at me, wondering why I would be so stupid.

"You don't want to go out?"

No please I want affection.

"This has been a hard day on you, I bet."

Yes, oh yes, very hard.

I walked back upstairs and sat on the rug in my bedroom near the heating vent. She walked in a circle, once, twice, and laid on the rug. She lowered herself in such a way that she leaned against my leg.

I placed my hand on her abdomen and rubbed, and then her shoulder and rubbed, and then her back and rubbed.

Yes, oh thank you, I feel better already.

She fell asleep soon but I stayed by her side another hour.

Mackenzie August, super softy.

16

The following morning, I inspected the house for dog hair. Even I, trained detective, found none. Maybe boxers shed less than other dogs, and shed short hairs at that?

Georgina Princess Steinbeck and I drove Kix to Roxanne's. Kix thought a dog being in the car was even more entertaining than Chuggington. I worried he might hyperventilate.

Afterwards, I stopped at Kroger for dog food and then she and I went to the office. She smelled everything and expressed approval at my masculine potpourri. She ate then and laid near the creaking water radiator and emanated contentment and I enjoyed it all. A well behaved dog was a delightful companion, turns out. Who knew.

I gazed at her, channeling all my years of experience and intuition. I thought and I deduced and I unraveled and I stewed. Reveal your secrets, animal. What part do you play in this mess? Impart unto me thine answers.

Nothing happened.

I would take her to Ulysses soon. Slight chance seeing

the animal would knock loose some hidden memory. Maybe bring him peace. But I doubted it. More work needed to be done.

The door downstairs banged open. Quick footfalls on the steps and then a girl in my doorway. Not a girl, more like a young woman. Nineteen? Twenty? She wore heeled leather boots and black leggings and an unzipped parka. Beneath the parka, a white shirt far too revealing. She was thin and shivering and her mousy brown hair was held back with gold clips. She brought with her a rush of chilly air.

Georgina glared suspiciously.

"You're Mr. Mackenzie, right," said the girl. Not really a question. She breathed heavily and her cheeks had pink spots. "Miss Veronica said I could run here. I need a place to sit."

"I am and you can."

She was already in. Glanced down the stairs. Went to the corner and stood. Made herself small.

I noted, "That's not sitting."

"Just a few minutes. Then I'll go, I promise. You aren't mad? Miss Veronica said I could."

"There's no rush. Is someone terrifying about to charge up the stairs? A politician, perhaps?"

No response. Still breathing heavily.

The door downstairs banged a second time. Heavier footsteps. The girl's face turned white.

I stood.

Georgina stood.

A man paused in the doorway. Old boots, baggy jeans, baggy Steelers jacket, new Steelers ball cap. Slab cheeks, needed a shave. He glanced at me. Glanced at the dog. Acknowledged us with a jerk of his head. From his spot, he couldn't see the girl cowering in the corner.

"Yo, you seen a girl run this way? Looking for my sister."

"No girls."

He looked some more. Thought about coming in.

Georgina growled.

The man jerked his head again. "Aight," he said.

He moved down the hallway, glancing into other offices —two accountants and a travel agent. We heard his heavy boots on the stairs, trudging to the third floor. Nothing up there but locked doors. By the sound, he tried them. Forcefully. Came down the stairs again. Slowly walked the halls. Stopped in my doorway again. Thought more about coming in.

Georgina growled again.

And something in my face said I was more dangerous than the dog.

I said, "What's your name? I see a girl running around, I'll tell her her brother's looking."

He didn't reply. Instead he said a very inappropriate word, went down the steps, and the door banged a third time. I walked across my office to verify his departure.

I looked at the girl. She looked back. "All clear."

She nodded. Looked like someone who just won a battle but fought in a hopeless and pyrrhic war.

"Sit. Any friend of Miss Veronica is a friend of mine," I said.

"Thanks, mister. I should go."

"Just a few minutes. I need you to pet my dog."

"Yeah, okay, I can do that. Sure." She sat on the chair and held her hand out. She wore three rings and chipped red nail polish. Georgina Princess consented to be petted. With abandon. "I like your dog, mister. What's it's name?"

"Georgina."

She smiled. "Good girl, Georgina. You got a rich person's name, don't you. Good girl."

"Who's the guy?"

"That guy? He's so stupid. That's Elton. Elton the felon."

"He's supposed to be protecting you. He protects you and you two split the profits."

Her mouth pressed into a grim line. "Don't know what you're talking about, mister. Miss Veronica said you're like a cop but not really. Said you don't try to fuck nobody."

"Might get that etched into my door. Good slogan. Why's Elton the felon mad at you?"

"Supposed to be working but I'm not," she said. She used both hands to scratch Georgina on the rump. "He wants money anyway. How'm I supposed to give him money if I'm not working? Stupid Elton."

"Who does Elton report to?"

"I don't know, mister. Nobody, maybe."

This was the problem Ronnie mentioned—no one looked after the girls. Parts of our society remained in the Dark Ages. The cold little human sitting on my chair, that was Ronnie's passion; a girl with a broken childhood, a girl trying to make ends meet the only way she knew how, and getting beaten up for it.

I read once that Jesus said, 'The poor you will always have with you.' I bet he would've said the same thing about prostitutes. Couldn't solve that problem. Ronnie knew that. But she wanted to protect them as best she could.

I slid my card across the desk, along with a twenty. "Go eat. Go sleep. Call Miss Veronica or me if Elton hurts you."

She glared glumly at the money. "Why're you giving me that?"

"I'm sweet on Miss Veronica. And she likes you."

"You two screwing?"

"Exclusively."

"Shit, I didn't know that." She stood and took the money and the card. "You're really big, mister. But Elton is mean."

"I can be meaner," I said. "If Miss Veronica asks me to."

∾

I HAD two months of office work glaring hatefully on my desk. So I spent the rest of the day sending invoices, paying bills dated in November, making phone calls, answering emails. And, because it was torture, drinking Johnnie Blue.

Georgina did not think my lifestyle compelling.

We went home at three. The sun was out, heating the earth to a balmy fifty degrees, so I put a leash on Georgina and decided to walk to Roxanne's. Waste not, want not, and that included vitamin D.

We lived on a corner lot and hidden just behind a row of boxwoods was a gigantic army personnel carrier, parked half on the street and half on my lawn. It was yellow and capable of carrying at least sixteen...

Ah, it was Gordon Gibbs in his H2. The vacuous husband of Colleen, ex-wife of Ulysses.

He saw me. I saw him. He saw me seeing him. He glowered. It was titillating.

He got out and slammed the Hummer door. Rolled his shoulders forward and puffed up to make himself bigger, like a puffer fish. He didn't need to puff up—the guy was humongous. Dressed head to toe in Nike, including a headband.

A headband! Wow.

"That's my dog," said Gordon Gibbs.

Georgina watched him curiously, wondering why a man his size and age wore short shorts.

"This dog? Yours? The heck you say."

"I knew you'd find it."

"*Her.* Who on earth would ever call a dog *it*?"

"Whatever, Mack. I knew you'd steal it and I knew if I came by a couple times I'd see you walking it."

"*Her.*"

He rolled his eyes. "The dog belongs to me."

"Tell me her name and she's yours."

"What?"

"Not repeating it. Do your best," I said.

"I don't know it's name. Who cares?"

"She does, you heartless monster with tiny calves."

His eyebrows inched upwards. "Tiny? I got more muscles in my calves than—"

"Look at them. So little."

"Calves are mostly genetic, asshole."

"Bad genes then? That's a shame," I said. "Surprised you don't fall over more."

"Give me the dog."

"Negative, chicken legs."

He pulled out his phone. "The dog's legally mine. You think I won't call the police? They'll throw your ass in jail so fast it'll make your head spin."

"Nope. None of that's accurate. Nothing in those three sentences is true. Call the police. You do, I'll give you ten bucks."

"I will."

I nodded encouragingly. "I got time."

He didn't.

His bluff was called.

His momentum stalled.

His complexion darkened.

I almost felt bad for him.

I said, "I'm curious. What would you do with the dog? Shake her until a million dollars fell out? Twist her like a Rubik's cube and when the pieces align a hidden door will pop open?"

"I don't know but I'll figure it out. If that asshole doctor wants it so bad, then the dog's worth something. Give it here."

"No."

"Fine. I'll take it from you," he said.

"With those legs? Hah."

"I can dead lift five hundred pounds, Mack. I do calf raises with—"

"Gordon, shut uuuup. I don't care. Your poor wife."

He stepped closer. He was bigger than me. Except for the calves. "I'll take it."

"Her. Go ahead."

He reached for the leash and I slapped his hand. He grunted and shoved me, but I rotated enough so he mostly missed and he staggered off balance.

"What are you doing, Gordon? Is this foreplay?"

He snatched the leash halfway down and said, "Hah. Got it. You're toast."

Georgina growled.

I smacked him. Open handed, across the face. My hand is large and strong and I caught him good, not a passing swipe but enough to raise a welt. Enough to hurt my hand. If his head was a bell, the sound would be heard for blocks. He let go and stumbled backwards. It stung. It stung a lot. His eyes watered.

"Are you worried the neighbors are watching and think you uncoordinated and clumsy? I would be," I said.

"You're messing with the wrong guy, Mack." Looked like he couldn't see straight.

"Thus far, evidence suggests you should be giving yourself this pep talk."

"I work out for a living. You think you'll win this fight?" He didn't want to be crying but he was. Sometimes you can't help the tears. Hard to come back from that, as a tough guy.

"I do. So does the hand print on your face."

"I don't want to kick your ass in public." He turned for the Hummer. Stumbled a little. "This isn't over. You gotta deal with me, asshole."

"Come back with new invectives, chicken legs. I'm tired of that one."

His Hummer roared and trundled away, picking up speed like a school bus.

Georgina and I considered one another.

"What makes you so valuable?"

I just am.

17

The next day.

The world endured.

I sat in my office. Georgina at the heating radiator.

I surfed the internet for Ulysses Steinbeck and found the accident three years ago, written up in the Roanoke Times. He'd been coming down Bent Mountain, reached the bottom—thankfully; otherwise he'd be dead—and careened off the road. The car plummeted less than ten feet; had he gone off at the top, he would've plummeted hundreds. He was hospitalized in critical condition.

I called the records office and requested the police report. I gave the woman the date and location of the accident and the driver's name as Ulysses Steinbeck. She'd have it for me in an hour.

Georgina and I left downtown and got on Highway 581, heading north. Following a hunch, we exited at Hershberger —lo and behold, the red light was burning at Krispy Kreme Donuts. Hot and fresh. We eased into the drive-thru, careful lest someone of consequence see our gluttony, and ordered a half dozen.

"Don't tell Ronnie," I said and I let Georgina have one.

Was I the best dog caretaker in the world? Or the worst?

A fine line I walk.

Roanoke County Police is in North Roanoke, off Cove Road. I let the dog remain in the car, windows cracked. She watched me go, alert and vigilant, ears tuned forward.

The nice lady in the records office didn't look at me or like me or do anything to warrant being called nice. She gave me the file and said, "You can't photocopy it."

"Take a photo with my cell phone?"

"No."

"Take it with me?"

"No."

"Wanna go on a date?"

"No."

"Fine, I'll pay."

"No."

I had two copies of the police report—the original with hand-written notes and the typed version.

May 12th. Officer Ingram arrived on site at 2:17am, southwest Roanoke County. Car went off Highway 221 approximately fifteen minutes prior. Woman had called for an ambulance and the ambulance arrived five minutes after Officer Ingram. Call originated from cell phone registered to Ulysses. Ulysses Steinbeck's name and address were listed, taken from his license. He drove an Audi—there was a dark photo of the car perpendicular with the ground, crunched, propped up by two trees, all windows broken. Audi totaled. I saw his insurance information and the car's registration. One witness—Verna Hardy drove by the wreck and she also called 911 before police arrived. Verna provided nothing of consequence. Ingram noted the night was warm, upper 70s, sky clear, almost a full moon. A picture taken from Google

Earth approximated the location of accident, and the officer drew an arrow indicating the direction the car had been traveling. Heading towards Roanoke, away from Floyd, like Ulysses was coming home. Ulysses badly hurt, unresponsive. Officer Ingram indicated he smelled alcohol.

Ingram was good, his report more thorough than most.

A note added later—blood work showed his BAC at 0.26. Jiminy Christmas, Ulysses. Takes hard work to get that drunk.

Ingram saved the best for last. At the bottom of his report—two women were traveling in the car with Ulysses. Neither had identification. Names were Regina George and Lacey Chabert. The two women wanted to follow the ambulance to Carilion Hospital, so they rode with Ingram. He listed their injuries as minor.

Ah hah. A clue! Turns out I could recognize one when I saw it. I'd begun to despair.

Ulysses had been traveling with *two* women, neither with ID. And I knew those names. Somehow. Somewhere.

I was stimulated.

If Georgina Princess Steinbeck had been in the car, Ingram would've written that down. I didn't expect she had been, but that would've been another clue.

I returned the police report and said, "Fascinating."

"Mmhm."

"Want a donut?"

The nice lady looked up from her computer. Not at me, but in my direction. "Krispy Kreme? Got extra?"

"I do if you let me make a photocopy."

She did not express amusement.

18

I wanted to call Carilion and ask about the two other women and their injuries, but HIPAA was a foe over which there could be no victory.

Instead I found the number for Officer Ingram, now a sergeant with Roanoke's K9 division.

"How about that," I told Georgina as I let her walk around the grass and do her business. "The K9 division. Your people."

Ingram agreed to meet me for lunch at Macado's, downtown. Macado's was a local chain with a large menu, cooked everything well, and over-decorated their walls with posters from movies, life-sized curios, and pictures of famous events. Ingram arrived in plain clothes. A short man, black, neat mustache, shaved head, serious expression.

"Off duty?" I asked.

"No. Just easier this way," he said. Polite but hard voice, as though he didn't want to be friendly in case he had to cuff me later. "Not everyone likes the blue, especially now days."

"That sucks."

"It does suck."

We ordered sandwiches and chips and ice water. I wanted a beer but knew he wouldn't.

"You're looking into the Steinbeck accident," he said.

"You remember it?"

"No one forgets something like that. Wasn't the last straw, but maybe second to last. Couldn't handle accidents anymore."

"Ulysses was in bad shape."

"Blood everywhere. Glass sticking out of his skull. Like someone jabbed big shards of windshield into his brain. He'd been thrown, bouncing around the tree trunks." Ingram shook his head, looking down. "Only so many memories like that I can handle."

"I worked homicide in Los Angeles, a while back."

"So you know," said Ingram.

"I know."

"Now you're private? Helping Steinbeck?"

"I am."

"Good for you."

I said, "You know he has amnesia."

"I visited him. Didn't remember me. What'd he hire you for?"

Our food came. He surprised me by saying grace before we tucked in.

A man of principle and faith and unafraid to express it. One day I'd be a fully functioning adult and might do the same.

Halfway into our sandwiches I said, "Steinbeck hired me to find his dog. But also he hired me to find out what was going on during that period of his life. He can't remember— he'd been acting out of character before the crash. The answers might bring some peace of mind."

And maybe two million dollars were at stake.

He wiped his hands with his napkin and drank water. "You want to know about the two women."

"I want to know about the two women."

He chuckled, though he didn't find it funny. "Regina and Lacey. I remember. Said they had no identification and I didn't feel like searching them. It was a bad night. So I let it go. Unprofessional, I realize."

"Were they torn up?"

"Yeah, beaten up bad but nothing broken. Not like Ulysses."

"Any guesses?" I said.

"Yeah. I got a guess."

"Prostitutes?"

"Don't think so. Didn't have the look. Again, just a guess. But I think one of the women was his daughter."

"Egads," I said. I was shocked. Hadn't expected that.

"On the report I wrote down 'woman.' She said she was twenty. But she wasn't," said Ingram. He finished his sandwich and played with the chips.

"Pretty girl? Blonde hair?"

"You got it. I met his ex-wife too. Don't remember her name, but they had a resemblance."

How about that. Alex Steinbeck had been in the car.

Mackenzie August, flabbergasted. Flummoxed. Poleaxed.

"Her name's Alex," I said. "Why would she lie about who she was?"

Spread his hands, palms up. "Got me."

"What about the second woman? Same age? Alex's friend?"

"No, older. Don't remember much about her appearance. Caucasian. Thin. Don't even recall her hair color. Like I said, rough night. Maybe his sister?"

"Doesn't have one. Rumors are, he had taken a lover."

He grinned. "Taken a lover."

"It helps sometimes if I talk like Sherlock Holmes."

"Does it? Maybe I should try."

"How long did you stick around?"

"At the hospital? Most of the night. Wrote up the report. Waited until the blood came back, for the BAC. Waited until his ex-wife arrived and I spoke with her."

"What happened to the two women? One of which presumably is Alex, his daughter."

He looked pained. Played with his chips some more. "Told you already, it was a rough night. And I wasn't professional enough. The two women left right before the ex-wife arrived. Intentional, I think, looking back. And then somehow, standing in the hall outside the operating room, the ex-wife crying and asking me what happened...I couldn't find the courage to tell her about two women being in the car with him."

"I don't blame you."

"I do. My superiors found out, they would."

"No dog in the car, right? At the scene of the accident?"

"No dog."

I sighed and rubbed at my forehead. "I need to talk to Alex again. About that night and the other woman and her involvement."

"She lied to me about something, could be obstruction."

"If she did, I'm not telling you. She's gonna hate me enough as it is."

"Why's that matter?" he asked. "She hates you or not?"

"I'm not sure. But it does. She's famous on Instagram."

"So?"

"Yeah I don't understand it either."

19

Tom Garrett didn't look like a mobster. He looked like he sold insurance. Thin guy, thick head of hair gone white and combed to the side. Maybe fifty-five, easy smile. Dressed in a suit and tie, big gold Auburn University ring. Gold tie clip, gold cufflinks. His loafers had tassels.

Ronnie, Marcus, and I met him in Staunton, an hour north of Roanoke and two hours south of Alexandria, where he lived. He reserved the entirety of a restaurant called The Shack. It was small, it was red, and it looked like a shack. Built on sloping South Coalter, not far from downtown.

Marcus brought Fat Susie and Tom brought his own body guard. They stayed at the cars talking about things enormous and muscular men talk about. Me, probably.

He shook my hand in a friendly manner and said, "I'm trying to be professional tonight, Mr. August, but it'll be a challenge. I'm a big fan."

"Call me Mackenzie. And why's that?"

"I watch the Gabbia Cremisi every year. A pack of us stream it live in my basement and place bets online. You had us glued. We screamed and shouted when the cot'-

damn lights went like you wouldn't believe. Lights come back on and pow, there was the Prince, lying on the ground like he was dead. You won me seventy-five grand."

Marcus Morgan made a grunting noise. "That's it? I got more."

Tom Garrett laughed, his face turning a little red and his eyes crinkling. "Thank God for the announcer, declaring you the winner, even as you fought in the crowd. Just a madhouse, am I right?"

"Provision from above," I said.

He didn't seem to hear. "I am absolutely attending the fights next year. The wife won't go and I let that stop me in the past, but to hell with that, right? Was it fun? It looked fun, I bet it was a blast, right?"

I debated kicking Tom between the legs.

Marcus said, "Would be fun 'sept we trying to save Mackenzie's ass."

"Oh he didn't need any saving. What'd they call you, the Yankee, right? The Yankee had it the whole way. You still got the tattoo?"

Ronnie smiled. "He does and I adore the name."

He laughed and winked. "I bet you do! Why wouldn't you?"

"What kinda business are you in, Tom?" I asked.

"Bank fraud! And boy is the business booming. I know I don't look like most of the other guys but I do my part. Well, I'll stop acting like a fan now. Or I'll try. C'mon on in—it doesn't look much but it's the finest dining this side of Richmond. Worth the trip."

I grabbed the door. Marcus went first.

Tom kissed Ronnie on the cheek and said, "Miss Summers, always a treat," and he followed Marcus.

Ronnie whispered to me, "I never slept with him. He's a family man. So cool it."

"Cool it?"

"Your hackles rose when he kissed me." She smiled. "I liked it."

"Liked the jealousy or the kiss?"

"I like you, now cool it," she said and we went in.

The restaurant had rustic charm, decorated as though one ate inside a remarkably clean barn. We sat in the middle of the empty room and two servers brought us pimento cheese with crackers and smoked whitefish dip. Tom and Marcus ordered an Old Fashioned, Ronnie a white wine, and me a beer.

"I took the liberty of ordering everything on the menu, I hope that's okay," said Tom. He had taken off his jacket and he rolled up his sleeves. He was so frangible he'd break if I slapped him like I'd slapped Gordon. "Mackenzie, one more question and then I'll relent, I promise—I gotta know, what happened in the dark with the Prince at the end?"

Ronnie placed her hand on my arm and squeezed. "In the dark, Mackenzie beat him senseless and stabbed him with the knife."

It was a lie. But she knew I didn't love the conversation and would soon beat Tom with his chair.

"Have you been paid yet?" he asked.

"In fact I have not. I wouldn't blame them if they didn't —we destroyed the hotel."

Tom frowned and shook his head. "That doesn't factor. No sir, that doesn't factor a lick. I'll look into it. I'll take care of it immediately, Mackenzie, trust me."

"Well thanks, Tom. But don't get yourself into a shouting match with the evil men of the world. I met them and they're unpleasant. It's only money."

He laughed and slapped the table. "It's only money! Listen to you, still got your sense of humor, I'll be doggone."

Marcus, reading my thoughts, grinned. "Tom here, he's about the money. Good ol' boy from the south, brings in cash. He's a big swinging dick with the Kings; not cause he's a tough guy but because he's smart."

"What kind of bank fraud do you handle?" I asked.

He looked pleased at the question. "I only fish the deep end of the pond, right? I go after the credit and identities of billionaires and siphon it away, little by little. Some are so rich they never suspect a thing, the fat bastards. But listen, Mack, if those Camorrista pricks want to keep doing business with the Kings, they'll pay the Gabbia Cremisi champion what he earned. I'll look into it, leave that to me."

Perhaps I'd judged Tom too hastily. Struck me as a real sweetheart.

We ate and more food came—salads and plates of short rib tartare and pork loins and pasta and guinea hen.

Tom ate his fill and brought out some papers. He passed them around for us to look at.

"I'll try to keep this simple, I know I can be a bore with financial details. The property and assets of Veronica Summers are hard to quantify, but I did my best. Look at the itemized list and alert me if anything is missing. I estimated her expenses from the last three years and came up with an average of $563,500."

Ronnie's fork paused on her plate. "You're kidding."

"That's enterprise wide, including things you never see, like..." He tapped his paper, indicating a column of numbers. "For example, fertilizer and taxes and interest and salaries and bribes and...you get the idea. This is based off paperwork submitted by Rueben Collier and Mr. Stokes and various bank records and receipts. Also I estimated revenue from the last three years and averaged it out to $2,480,100. Or at least, the expected revenue."

Ronnie's fork remained frozen. "Per year?"

"Yes. Two point four eight a year. Approximately."

"Where is all of it?"

"The business is a mess, right? Some of it's in a bank account. One in particular has four hundred thousand collecting dust and interest; Ruben makes deposits and withdrawals but you don't, probably because you don't know about it. Your late father was not an organized man, I believe, no offense and may he rest in peace. Some of it was poorly managed, some of it went to the Kings. As I said, that was the expected revenue, but the realized is less." Tom leaned back in his chair and finished his cocktail. Another was brought. "I was against this sale to begin with. Why mess with a good thing? But after examining the fiscal details the past two days, I've changed my mind."

"Why?" I asked.

"To be frank, the business isn't run well. Too many players skimming, too much money unaccounted for, not efficient enough, you get the idea. All the parts are there to be a well-oiled machine, right? But the parts don't connect effectively."

"All the more reason I should sell," said Veronica.

"I concur but it's tricky," he said.

"Why?"

"Because it's you," I said.

Tom nodded politely. "Because it's *her*. And because it's *you*, Mackenzie. Just about every sum'bitch I work with loves her. And just about all of them know about you. Hell, I'll say it—you won the tournament and you keep killing our guys. You're infamous. Kinda scary. I asked around before coming down. Even the Kings who like you, Mackenzie, think they're better off with you dead."

I said, "They're nervous about us getting out of the business entirely. Because once we're free, they'll have less control over things."

Tom nodded. "You hit the nail on the head. You're hotter than a Laramie parking lot."

"We're a loose end. I'm a loose end who is threatening to kill Darren Robbins and Ronnie's got incriminating evidence on half of them."

"You can see why the Kings prefer to be in business *with* you, rather than against you."

I said, "What if I back down on my promise to kill Darren? Would that ease everyone's mind?"

"It would help," he said.

"What if I killed him tomorrow and then we have this conversation again? Would that ease everyone's mind?"

Tom looked pained.

"Are you really going to murder Darren?" Ronnie didn't just look at me, she turned her whole body my direction. "That strikes me as wildly out of character."

"Unless someone convinces me otherwise. One of us will kill the other soon and I prefer to kick off rather than receive."

"But you're no hitman. Nor a common thug."

"Neither is the man threatening me."

"Darren cancelled the hit," said Tom.

"Darren's a prick and a coward and he can't exist for long with me roaming around. Could you? If I threatened you?"

"To be frank, Mackenzie, I'd have you aced, as they say. Even though I'm a big big fan."

"Exactly. And that's what Darren will do."

Tom looked even more pained.

Ronnie said, "None of this changes the fact that I want to sell the marijuana operation."

"Like I said, I'm in favor of the sale now," said Tom. "But it's tricky. On your end. Once you're out, there's less reason to let you live. That's the thinking of some of my business associates."

"The associates on whom she has no dirt," I said. "Those who are under her threat feel differently, I imagine."

Ronnie leaned forward. A candle on the table illuminated the underside of her jaw and neck, like a reverse shadow. "I'm done with it. Okay, Tom? I'm out. Let's do the sale and you can tell those fat old men not to worry. I don't want to blackmail, I don't want to leverage my way into more power, I'm through."

"I'll pass the message to my cohorts but you know what they'll say, Miss Summers."

"They'll grab their crotches and burp something about, 'She's out when we say she's out.'"

"Ah, well, yes. That's it."

She smiled the way lions smile at mice. "It's a fucking boys club. I know. And I was forced to play their game. But now I've got them by the balls. I have pictures and videos and audio and transcripts that'll get half of them killed or locked away. I'm not here to play, I'm here to take my stuff and go home. They've got a week to promise we're through or I release the incriminating evidence on Jerry Francis."

Tom's eyebrows rose. "Jerry Francis? You've got—? *The* Jerry? Wow. I didn't, I didn't know."

Ronnie nodded. Only a little. Although the candle on the table remained static, the fire burning in her eyes took on greater heat. "Jerry the Tranny Francis. Tell him I called him that. My video will ruin him. In one week. And then every month after that, I release another. If I die, they all get released at once to the Washington police, to the FBI, and to the media. Tell them that, Tom."

I leaned back in my chair and drank beer. Smugly.

Tom stood. Smoothed his tie and cleared his throat. He began sweating, tiny beads along the hairline. "One moment please. If you don't mind."

He went to the restroom.

I said, "He calling a cohort?"

Marcus nodded. Finished his Old Fashioned and beckoned for another. "Mmhm. Maybe two. Give them his impression of Summers's threat."

"He's a weak man." Ronnie's spine was straight, her shoulders thrown back. "Can't think for himself."

Marcus nodded a little. "Tom don't handle the violence. Just numbers. But he likes associating with those who do. A wimp? Yeah. Weak? Maybe not. More than he looks."

Tom returned sixteen minutes later. Sat down and scooted his chair forward. "I think the Kings will respect your wishes, Miss Summers, on reflection. Darren Robbins is a bridge we'll cross another day, am I right?"

"Yeah he is," I said. "Looking forward to that bridge. It's gonna be the best bridge."

"I suggest we continue with transactional details concerning Miss Summers's operation." He cleared his throat again and shuffled papers, bringing his mind back to task. "Should we?"

Ronnie and Marcus both assented

"As I said, your operation should be bringing in 2.4 million. It isn't, but it should. Having Marcus in charge should shore up the leaks. He's excellent at this, after all. One reason I'm in favor of the sale? Our cut will enlarge."

Without changing expression, Marcus toasted him with his new cocktail.

Tom continued, "We usually sell in the 2-4 EBIT range, and in this scenario I suggest the upper half because profit margins should increase. You wanted my professional evaluation, here it is. After examining the numbers, I propose a sale price of $8,425,000."

Marcus nodded without comment.

In my head, I was already shopping for a new pair of sneakers. Mine were two years old.

"That's too high," said Veronica. I remained calm. "I'm not doing this for money, I'm doing this to get out. Marcus risked his life to save my husband just because I asked. I came here hoping Mr. Garrett would give me a number close to three million and, considering he exceeded the number, I'll take three and a half."

I debated telling her that if she took eight million I could upgrade my Honda Accord, but it didn't seem the time.

Marcus said, "Summers, you—"

She reached for his hand. Squeezed. Even professional stoics and happily married men like Marcus Morgan get quiet when Veronica Summers touches them. She said, "It's complex, Marcus. But I'm not interested in maximizing my potential profit and I'm not interested in haggling with you. I want you to have it because you're responsible and you care about me and my husband and you care about Roanoke. In a perfect society we get rid of the drugs. Until then, it's better if men like you handle them. Plus I'm putting every penny of it into a woman's shelter. I've already picked out the building downtown. I'm taking care of girls. Prostitutes. I don't care if they quit the job or not, that's up to them. But I want to run a safe place they can stay. And three million is plenty."

Tom looked pained, the poor creature. He did that often.

Marcus said, "Gotta be more than three, Summers."

With her free hand she tapped the white table cloth, her red fingernail clicking firmly. "I am intentionally and willfully taking less. I am expressing to you and to myself what I think about money. I don't need wealth. I want to help hurting women like me and this is enough to start."

"I'll give you six."

Ronnie ceased her response even as she drew breath. I saw the conflict in her. Despite her speech, she liked wealth. A lot. She had several hundred grand hanging in her closet. This must be half killing her.

I whispered, "Take the six. Imma buy Nikes."

"Shut up, August," said Marcus. "I'll buy you Nikes."

"No, *I'll* buy him Nikes. For the rest of his life. He married me, not you."

Either way, I got new shoes. So all was well.

Finally Ronnie said, "I know myself, Marcus. That amount is too much. It'll kill me."

Marcus shifted in his chair. Glanced at the three of us. "I'll give you two now. Cash. And then another million each of the next three years. Final offer."

She made a cute face, drawing her mouth to one corner. Postulating. "Okay. Deal. And I'll name the shelter The Marcus Morgan Home For Whores."

"You do and I'll have to move. And take August with me."

She laughed. He laughed. I laughed.

Tom looked pained.

MARCUS DROPPED us off at my house late that evening. We strolled the sidewalk, her leaning against me. Her heels clicked with each footfall and I enjoyed it.

I stopped her on the front porch.

"You just turned down millions of dollars."

"I know." She made a slight groaning sound. "Don't remind me. I still can't feel my legs. I've wanted to be wealthy my entire life."

"Do you know why you did?"

"Yes. I'm growing up, I hope. I've grown up enough to realize I'm not an adult yet, at least not one that functions well. And if I became rich, I'd spiral into a black hole I'd never get out of. You don't give an idiot a license to practice law and you don't give a mess like me millions of dollars. And here's the best part, Mackenzie. I didn't do it for you. I did it for me."

"Wow."

She pushed some blond hair from her eyes. "Right? How august and pious am I? I'm essentially the Pope."

I grinned and got the door for her.

"Let's go in and talk about money and pretend we already have it, because..." She smiled and I nearly tripped. "Because what could be more fun than that? Other than sex with one another. This is why I rejected it, because just the thought makes me tingle. I'll need some way to launder the money so it looks legal. Two million at once is a lot, after all. Suspicious as all get out."

Georgina Princess Steinbeck greeted us.

My attention drifted as Ronnie talked.

Laundering money.

Laundering money.

Hmmm.

A few chimes were ringing in my head.

But I had no idea why.

Par for the course.

20

Courtney Farmer got on her knees when I entered her animal hospital the next morning, and she threw her hands out. Georgina Princess abandoned all pretense at self-possession and bounded to her, the leash pulling out of my grip. How do dogs intuitively know that vets love them?

Perhaps it was the posture of lowering oneself to their level.

Courtney and Georgina spent half a minute letting the other know how highly she was valued and then we ventured deeper into the hospital.

"A beautiful boxer," she said. She remained a tall and trim vet with shoulder length brown hair dyed blond and eyes a fraction too wide, as though surprised or impressed. I picked Georgina up and set her on the examination table. "Just perfect, yes she is. Yes she is. You two are ideal together, Mackenzie, like a commercial. I'd buy whatever you're selling. Gonna tell me what I'm looking for, big guy?"

"No," I said. "Render unto her the most thorough inspection possible and tell me if you see anything spectacular or amiss."

Georgina submitted to the examination with grace and dignity and enthusiasm.

"She's eating?"

"Yes," I said.

"What do you feed her?"

"Not beer and donuts, that's for sure."

"Drinking plenty of water?"

"Yes."

"Breathing fine? Energy is good? Have you witnessed bowel movements?"

"I have; best thirty seconds of my day. Healthy dog poop, no doubt."

"You brought a sample?"

I handed her the brown bag, inside of which there was a sealed plastic bag, inside of which there was a small sealed Tupperware container, inside of which there was a small stool sample, which was gross.

She and Georgina talked about some things, checking hearing and alertness. She and Georgina trotted around the room. She checked the skin on her belly—Georgina's belly —and looked in her eyes and ears and nose, and she pulled her lips up and looked at her teeth, which was also gross. She palpated the legs and lymph nodes and abdomen. With a stethoscope she auscultated the heart and lungs, talking softly to herself.

Courtney took x-rays while I made soothing sounds for the sake of the canine and she used an ultrasound wand to look everywhere else. I watched the garbled feed on the monitor as she pointed out organs and I learned nothing.

After forty-five minutes of rigorous scrutiny, and after the stool was witnessed under a microscope, Courtney set Georgina upright, gave her a treat and pronounced, "Health-iest three-year-old boxer imaginable. I love her to pieces and she's got a sweet temperament. Patient and calm and she adores you. So what gives? Ulysses Steinbeck ordered all this?"

"No. He doesn't know I have the dog yet. Before I tell him, I was hoping you'd find something."

Courtney Farmer looked at me as if I had mange. "Find something? Give me more details. Like what?"

"A tumor worth two million dollars? Pot of gold in her intestines? A femur shaped like a skeleton key? I don't know. Do you see any indications of trauma? She was wounded when Ulysses first got her."

"No. I see nothing but a perfect dog."

I sighed and patted Georgina. "She's a puzzle piece that doesn't fit."

"Maybe it's you who needs his head examined, not her."

"A bizarre diagnosis, doctor. But potentially accurate."

GEORGINA LAID on her side on my passenger seat as though the doctor's visit exhausted her. Head down, eyes closed. I drove her home, the winter sunlight blinking through the window and turning her fur aureate.

I patted her for the duration, experiencing an odd form of guilt.

Farmer was right—this was an exceptional dog, seemed to me. Put up with a lot, no complaints, obeyed all the rules, wasn't shedding. A puzzle piece she may be, but also more than that. And impossibly likable.

We parked in my driveway and idled, and I scratched at her ribs, burrowing my fingers beneath the fur and rubbing against skin and ribs, and scratched and scratched, and she was pleased. I got her shoulder and her neck and her chest and her haunch, and she laid without moving in the sparkling sun and soaking the heated seat's warmth. The light came through in such a way that she reflected the brilliance but also absorbed it, and as I scratched her fur I could see skin under the dense growth. I rubbed the side of her abdomen this way and that, parting the fur like a wave.

During such a wave I saw markings on her skin but the fur immediately closed overtop. So brief it could be imagination. Scar from the old wound? I placed both hands on her and used my thumbs to draw the fur aside. Her hairs were short and stiff and uncooperative, but she didn't mind.

With careful manipulation I found the marking again. Multiple markings—it was a pale blue tattoo. I'd seen these before; vets used the same ink to indicate a neutered animal. But vets marked the animal's belly, not the side. I shifted Georgina enough to get direct sunlight and pushed her fur aside. After enough iterations of the glimpses, the hidden marking resolved into patterns and I knew what I was looking at.

Numbers. Georgina Princess Steinbeck's abdomen had been tattooed with at least ten numbers.

21

Georgina remained placid on the warm seat for twenty minutes while I scrutinized her abdomen. The numbers were tiny and they'd grown distorted as she aged. Some of the numbers I had to guess at. Was that a 1 or a 7? Eventually my thumbs and eyes were raw, and I relented and sat up to examine my phone, where I'd written down my best guesses.

371612

-801716

Who on earth would tattoo a dog thusly?

Someone who didn't care about dogs.

Someone like Ulysses. This was the key mentioned in his journal. These numbers were what his subconscious clawed at. He'd forgotten the dog, forgotten the numbers, but some part of him remembered the necessity of them.

Be nice if he could remember what the numbers symbolized but I bet he forgot. On some level, this was what I'd been hired to do.

I was supposed to parlay with him that afternoon, but I

texted Rose Bridges and informed her I needed to delay the meeting.

A clue had surfaced, after all, and needed decoding. And I, Sherlock Holmes.

GEORGINA and I went walking and I thought.

I went to the gym to exercise and I contemplated.

I made a late lunch and I postulated.

I punched the numbers into Google and got nothing back. I subtracted them. I sent them to Manny. I translated the numbers into letters. Nothing. I changed the 1s into 7s and tried it again. I put it all on paper, including the name Georgina Princess. I rearranged, I deciphered, I codified.

I traveled to the city library and showed them to a librarian, but they made no sense even to an expert at the dewey decimal system. I called Whitney Potter and asked if the arrangement made sense to a physician, but they didn't. I stopped by my bank but the manager indicated these weren't routing or account numbers.

The numbers weren't zip codes or telephone numbers. They weren't patents. Potentially Bitcoins or some other blockchain currency, but it looked doubtful. Not credit card numbers, not social security numbers, not passport IDs.

That evening I stared at the numbers on a pad while I chopped onions and garlic for chili. The secret to my chili, as with many other things, was bacon. I sautéed the onions and garlic in bacon grease, emptied the pan into the pot with the beef and beans and tomato sauce and Rotel, and stirred and set the lid on top. I got a Dogfish Head brown, popped the top, and watched Georgina walk circles around Kix's playpen and Kix try to keep up from within. They had a good thing going—Kix would throw plastic blocks and Georgina would bring them back, stick her mouth over the side, and release the block. Not hygienic, probably. But Courtney Farmer had let the dog lick her on the face and mouth—ew—so I didn't panic.

Timothy August returned. He petted Georgina politely, and picked up Kix and they hugged one another and inquired after the other's day. Then Kix was returned. Timothy hung his coat up and set his briefcase on the stairs. He clapped me on the shoulder and washed out his coffee mug before getting a scotch glass and pouring himself two fingers worth.

"Smells good," he said, walking to his reading chair.

"Obviously. Ready in forty-five minutes."

"Are you geocaching tomorrow? Too cold, in my learned opinion."

"Did you say geocaching?"

"I did," said Timothy August.

"That game where people hide treasures for each other under rocks and bears and so forth."

"Correct." He sat in the chair and drank scotch and closed his eyes. Kix called to him, and he smiled and waved and Kix waved back.

"Why would I be geocaching tomorrow?"

"Aren't those the coordinates for Roanoke? On your notepad?"

I looked at the numbers. I looked at him. With keen insight sharpened from years in homicide and years more as a private investigator, I said, "Huh?"

"A science teacher at Crystal Spring Elementary is big into geocaching. He makes me listen to his exploits and look at the GPS coordinates on his map. I thought that's what you had there. I must be mistaken."

I said, "What are the coordinates for Roanoke?"

"Thirty-seven point something, and negative eighty point something. Right? Isn't that what you have written down?" He drank more scotch and closed his eyes again. "Or maybe ignore me, an old man yammering after a long day. I couldn't find enough subs so I taught music class, and there's not enough Glenlivet in the world."

I glared some more at the numbers.

371612

-801716

I drew a dot after the 7 and after the 0.

37.1612

-80.1716

I opened my laptop and surfed to a website that mapped latitude and longitude, and I entered the coordinates. The map flickered and zoomed in on southwest Roanoke County.

Only five miles from the location of Ulysses's car crash.

"Jiminy Christmas," I said.

Dad opened his eyes. "Was I helpful?"

"You're right. These are map coordinates. On Bent Mountain, near the site of his car accident."

"I should be a sleuth. August and August, Father and Son Sleuthing Agency."

"Want to hear the darnedest thing?"

"I do."

"Georgina Princess Steinbeck. Her initials are GPS. Global Positioning. How about that."

Kix laughed. *Took you long enough.*

22

That night I sat upright in bed, ankles crossed, listening to Manny snore on my floor, and I made a list of things I didn't know.

Why was Alex Steinbeck at the sight of her father's crash, and why did she lie to the police about it?

Why had Steinbeck tattooed a puppy with GPS coordinates?

What was at that spot on the map? Because according to the satellite images, it was nothing but a massive expanse of forest.

Did this have anything to do with his mental breakdown? I mean, it sounded like something a crazy guy would do.

Who was the mysterious woman at the crash? Had to be a paramour. Or his ex-wife. Or his daughter's friend. Or somebody I hadn't met yet. Or Salma Hayek, which would be my first choice.

Was Colleen Gibbs as innocent as she seemed?

What about the shady and sudden trip to the casino? How did this factor into everything?

And the last question was, what was I being paid to do? The easiest answer—find the dog. Done! But Ulysses also requested I find out why the dog was important. Done! Mostly! Kinda!

Here you are, Ulysses, here's the dog and here are the GPS coordinates tattooed on the dog's ribcage. Have a nice life.

That wouldn't work. He didn't *want* the dog.

And he'd immediately ask me to divine the significance of the GPS coordinates.

So maybe I should do that.

It's nice to have a purpose in life.

Georgina Princess Steinbeck whined in her sleep and sighed from her spot near the heating vent, two feet from Manny's head. A curious characteristic of mine—lonely people and/or dogs sleep on my floor.

Downstairs, someone came in the front door. Locked it. That someone kicked off her heels and ascended the stairs.

Here comes the lady. O so light of foot,
Will ne'er wear out the everlasting hardwood.

She entered and her face blossomed with gladness and, stepping over Manny with her dainty bare feet, she laid two large aluminum briefcases on my mattress.

She said, "We're rich," and her chest, neck, and cheeks flushed.

These violent delights have violent ends.

I said, "The sale is finalized?"

"I signed everything Tom Garrett sent me and Marcus brought the money." She inserted a key into the briefcases and they clicked and the lid opened. "Mackenzie, just look."

Stacks and stacks of hundred dollar bills. Stacks and stacks of twenties. They overflowed the secure case and spilled onto my comforter.

Even I, conservative and spartan, experienced a rumble of pleonexia like thunder in my gut.

"The wildest part," she said, caressing the cash, "is that I already spent ten thousand. And look what's left."

Manny murmured and shifted.

I said, "Did you purchase an entire season of box seats at the Salem Red Sox?"

"I did not, silly."

"Then you wasted ten thousand."

"I spent it on clothes, including many items best described as lavish lingerie."

"As it turns out, you are a wise capitalist."

"I skipped work today, Mackenzie." She perched on the side of the bed and rested her shoulder against mine. "Clients are mad at me. The windfall is already making me lazy and I can't stop thinking about ways I want to waste a million. This is a disaster waiting to happen. No, this is a disaster already occurring, and in slow motion."

"Should we spread it out and fool around on top?"

"I cannot imagine anything less hygienic. Is the cash arousing you?"

I said, "No, you arouse me. But I perceive it's an aphrodisiac for you and I hope to benefit."

"With Manny in the room?"

"And the dog."

She smiled the smile of a women pleased with her husband's pursuit, but unwilling to be caught for a few moments more. Patience and promise. She stood and looked down at the money and briefcase and thoughtfully sucked at her lower lip. "I need to dispose of this to my finance guy soon. I am unable to be trusted."

"Probably wise."

"But first I should invest in some Louboutin heels."

"Almost certainly."

"And a Gucci purse I've been eyeing since last year."

"Where else would you keep all your money?" I said.

"Lynsey told me you helped her."

"Lynsey?"

"A girl I know. Local prostitute. She said you protected her from Elton," she said.

"Lynsey? Are you intentionally avoiding the D in her name?"

"Lynsey. Without the D."

"Elton the felon," I said. "I met him. Seems like the worst kind of pimp."

"He is. I despise Elton. I want to kill him."

"He offer to take you on?"

"He suggested I could make a lot of money, yes."

"Then I'll kill him for you free of charge."

Another fond look at the money, balanced in equipoise between greed and growth. She arranged the loose stacks of cash into the aluminum briefcases. The pressure spilled them out again, so she used one hand to push and the other to arrange and lower the lid, a delicate operation.

"Can I hire you tomorrow?" she said. "Your services as a private cop? To talk with Elton. Should take less than an hour."

"Pimps aren't entirely without function. The protection and collection services he provides are most likely genuine."

She turned her attention to the other briefcase and said, "Wow, this is sexy. I like simply touching the stuff." She ran her thumb over the end of a stack of hundreds, like a poker dealer shuffling cards. "I know Elton provides a service. But I propose he does more harm than good. Trust me, Mackenzie, this is my purview."

"Happy to speak with Elton. No payment required."

Finished packing, she set both cases on the floor and raised to look at me. Smiled a smile born of many joys. "None?"

"Well. Perhaps the aforementioned lingerie?" I said.

THIRTY MINUTES LATER, as we drifted towards slumber, intertwined, she whispered against my shoulder, "Don't divorce me yet, Mackenzie. I'm rich now."

She was asleep seconds after.

23

Elton the felon lived in an apartment downtown off Church, near the YMCA. It rained last night and puddles remained on the sidewalks but the air had warmed so my wait was bearable. He emerged from the locked lobby at 9:15am. Same sneakers, same baggy jeans, same cockeyed ball cap. With his left hand, he spoke into his phone. With his right, he fished out a pack of cigarettes.

I took the phone away from him and disconnected the call and said, "Ah man, they hung up on you."

He dropped the pack of cigarettes. Essayed an expression of anger and disbelief at my stupidity. "The hell are you?" He said it like *hay-el.*

"We talk, Elton the felon, and then I return your phone." I slid it into my pocket.

Elton had grown up rough. He bore the scars, even if they weren't visible. I could probably recite his own major childhood events to him, I'd heard them so often from others; the abuse menu wasn't that long. A hit or be hit world, that's what he knew. It wasn't fair to him as a child and it wasn't fair now but sometimes we dealt with things that are instead of things that should be.

Elton hit me. Hit or be hit.

Candid videos of people fighting on the street are always awkward. It's not like a boxing match where professionals generate nine hundred pounds of force, expertly placed. Videos of angry amateurs on the street show fighters throwing punch after punch, ineffectual, and neither man dropping. Because the hits don't land and the punches lack stopping power and zeal. Eventually the guys are tired and distressed and they allow themselves to be separated.

Elton hit me in such a way. It wasn't good. He wanted to rattle me, impress me with his willingness to inflict damage. But the blow was glancing and there was no shoulder behind it and he was already gathering for another punch, even worse than the first. My lip might bruise a little, that was it. After Italy, this felt like a game.

"Elton, be serious. Let's talk instead. I promise not to diagnose the infelicities of your technique."

He came again, trying to go up and over my shoulder. Some neglectful combination of a jab and cross. Cursing too.

I hit him in the stomach as it should be done. Not the first in a series of wild strikes but one concentrated blast. I hit him with everything I had, down to my heels, up to my shoulder, driving my fist almost to his spine via his navel.

He went onto his knees and he made a few gagging noises and then vomited.

I winced. "You ate Oreos for breakfast?"

A couple walking by on the far sidewalk saw us. They paused, compelled on a subterranean level to do *something*. Intervene? Call the police? Separate us?

The woman asked the man, "Should we...?"

The man glared. He wasn't a violent man, he wore loafers through puddles for goodness sake, and he didn't want to bother, and so he glared.

"C'mon," he told her. "Let the riffraff kill each other."

I waved and smiled.

They kept walking, assuring themselves it was for the greater good.

And it was.

I crouched beside Elton and said, "Were they double stuffed? The Oreos?"

He wiped his mouth.

"Fucking kill you..." Turned suddenly on his knees, pivoting at the waist, and tried to hit me again.

I pushed his hand aside, balled a fist, and hit him on the nose. Hard enough to crunch cartilage, hard enough to hurt, and not break bone.

The woman kept watching us over her shoulder as they marched quickly up the sidewalk. The man scolded her to stop peeking.

I said, "I only want to talk, Elton. Try again, I'll bop your nose harder.

He said something unintelligible into the hand holding his nose. He needed a shave and a shower and a stick of deodorant. Needed to wash his clothes. Needed to eat some fruit and vegetables and scrub his face at night with soap and a washcloth. He needed to take better care of his teeth and stop smoking. He needed a mother.

"I got a feeling you're gonna try again, Elton the felon. The way you grew up, that's all you got. The only thing that works. But it won't right now. You're violent but not good at it. Your violence is only effective against people smaller or tamer than you. I'm neither. And I've been trained. I'll smack you around all day and not breathe heavy. Police show up? I'll tell them what you do for a living. Fighting is lose-lose for you. So let's talk, huh?"

I saw the rage and fear shrink a little as he listened. Maybe I wouldn't hurt him anymore. Maybe he didn't have to act tough for a few minutes.

"Here's what it is. You're a pimp. You arrange meetings between girls and the local cooks at the restaurants downtown, and the guys working at nearby garages, and the custodians coming off shift, and the night guards, and the construction crews, maybe some of the hospital staff, and others I haven't thought of. Quick encounters, nothing fancy; many days your job is easy. Probably a handful of others like you around because seventy-thousand people work in and around downtown, and they have sexual needs like everyone else and they choose this particular path. For the moment, let's not moralize. Let's deal with what is. If you quit, they go to the next guy. It's gonna happen and I'm not here to make you stop. We doing okay so far?"

Elton remained cagey and aloof.

"So why am I here? To help you see reason. The job you're in is hard enough without being mean. Being mean hurts you and it hurts the girls. You need to learn that your girls are prettier when you don't hit them. That their lives will have more meaning if they feel valued. That business will be better if everyone is happy. That this world is a big cruel vacuum sometimes and we got to fight against it, and one way to do that is to reduce the suffering of others whenever possible."

He did a scoffing sound and blood spattered from his nose onto his shirt. "Man, I don't know who the fuck you are." With his clogging nose, it sounded like *Bad, I don know who da fug you dar.* "But you sound like a bad after school special. And you don't know nothing about me or about whores."

"I know more than you think I do."

He did the scoffing sound again.

I said, "I know you can't admit it now. Tough guys like you don't have that button. But you need to become more. More than you are now, for the sake of the girls you watch. And for your sake. Because the real reason I'm here? Is to manipulate your behavior, Elton the felon. I'm not going anywhere. And I'll come back to visit you soon if you keep hitting people. I like this city and I don't like it when guys hit girls who live here. And I'll make you stop, Elton. I promise."

As I stood he made an awkward kicking motion at me, like a petulant child. I dropped the phone into his lap.

"Next time I break your nose and the hand you used to hit the girl," I said and I walked down Church, hung a left on 4th, and got into the driver's seat of my car.

Ronnie sat in the passenger. She wore a grim expression.

"He's not done being mean. We'll have to visit him again, my guess. You watched?"

She nodded.

I said, "Because you want to know what'll be required to affect change in the prostitution industry."

She nodded again. She rested her right elbow on the car door's window ledge and leaned against her knuckles. Stared through the windshield into nothing. She filled the car with the aroma of shampoo and Burberry perfume.

Ronnie was in her mid-thirties. She looked late-twenties, but sometimes her soul groaned if you listened close enough and you realized she felt ancient some days.

After a period of silence, she said, "This is why marriage vows are important."

Caught off guard. Wasn't expecting that. "Yeah?"

"Because if you're married to me, Mackenzie, you know I might ask you to do things like this now and then. To stop someone, or to hurt someone, and it's a risk. And if we're bound together then you'll feel obligated. So you've got to be asking yourself...do you want to be bound to me? You never got to make the decision. I made it for you."

Do you want to be bound to me? I *did* want to—that was never the question. Better phrased as, *should* you? Should I be bound to her?

I started the car and drove to her office, where she'd left her red Mercedes. I parked behind it and she placed her right hand on my passenger car door's interior handle and paused.

She said, "I'm in my head about this, I know."

"You're taking us seriously. It's better for both of us that way, I think."

"I have counseling later. I need her advice. About the cash in the briefcases. And our potential annulment." The word annulment didn't make it out in one piece. She took a shuddering breath and looked away.

"Ronnie."

"Yes Mackenzie."

I took her hand and squeezed. "We never decided to annul."

"But we should."

"If we do, an annulment doesn't mean we break up. It means we plan to do things right."

"It feels like you're drifting away from me."

"But am I?"

"It's just the years of loneliness and fear and insecurities talking. I know it is. But that doesn't make it stop."

"Years of abuse aren't conquered in mere weeks. Rome wasn't built in a December."

She was crying now. "Don't break up with me, Mackenzie, not yet. Kay? I'm trying to be good. It's just...harder than I thought."

"I'm not breaking up with you."

"But you *should*. Don't you get that?"

"You think I'm sitting here weighing you on a scale. Creating lists of pros and cons and judging you. But I'm not."

"I'm judging myself."

"Then go easy. Make sure you lump all the crap you've conquered into the pros and forgive yourself the rest."

She squeezed my hand. Released and wiped her eyes. "I'm a fucking lunatic."

She opened the car door and stood. Smoothed her clothes, closed the door, took her bag from her car, and walked toward her office.

A few other women arrived and walked the short sidewalk with her. Veronica Summers looked like a different species. Tall, strong, graceful. She shined on a cloudy day. She walked better in heels than the other women did in rain boots, and they knew it, and they watched her the way cubs would observe the tigress. She laughed and tossed her hair and went in, master of the universe.

I'm trying to be good.

A fool's errand. A destination constantly retreating and beyond reach.

What fools we mortals be.

What broken insecure messes in need of redemptive love. And I wasn't talking about her.

24

I left my office at eleven.

Hiking boots? On.

Windbreaker? Zipped.

Phone? Charged.

Jaw? Prominent and fixed in determination.

Clues? None.

But I was about to change that.

I hadn't made it three blocks before I saw Gordon Gibbs tailing me. Did he think he could hide in a Hummer the size and color of a small school bus?

Poor guy. He was trying his darndest.

In my Honda I turned right on Jefferson, then right on Salem, right on Market, and another right on Campbell, going in a full circle. He did his best, running stoplights, cutting off pedestrians, trying to stay inconspicuous three cars back. I executed the same routine again and this time he failed. His enormous tank got blocked by a party of hipsters moving slow and on their phones, allowing two additional cars to pull out, allowing a third to try and parallel park, and by the time he got free I was long gone.

Turns out, Gordon was a lot closer to the truth than I expected him to be. He thought Georgina Princess held keys to some secret. Lo and behold, she did. Gordon's gut had proved correct. Even a blind squirrel driving a Hummer, I supposed, finds an acorn now and then.

GPS was with Kix and Roxanne, and Roxanne had firm directions to call me and the police if she saw a big yellow Hummer at her door. Gordon would have to find some other acorn—he couldn't have mine.

I roared west into the county, got on 221, and left the hubbub behind. Instead of stores, there were homes. Instead of stoplights, hills. Out here lived accountants and doctors and lawyers and business owners who preferred land to social ascension. They wanted a view, not another invite to a swanky cocktail party.

Not judging city folk. I didn't want land either.

I passed the site of Ulysses's crash—debated stopping but nothing useful could be learned after three years of Mother Nature eroding evidence—and went up Bent Mountain. The road switched back again and again, carving up the side and offering views for twenty miles. Ulysses was lucky to be alive, piloting down this treacherous incline with hairpin turns while drunk. I turned off 221, now on small country roads, watching the map on my phone, taking wrong turns, and inching closer to my destination—a forest stretching for miles.

Soon I'd gone as far as I could. I parked off Bottom Creek Lane in a clearing of bare oak and poplar. Killed the engine and listened. I knew a couple farmhouses were nearby but I felt entirely alone. Just me and the trees.

I retrieved a backpack from the trunk, tightened it across my shoulders, locked the car, and set off. I followed Big Laurel Creek into the wilderness, steadily marching upward.

The undergrowth squished wetly, threatening to soak my boots and socks before long, but I stumbled across a bare path running parallel to the creek. Squirrels watched curiously and deer fled before me, the big stupid human stomping through Eden.

I hiked for an hour, eventually leaving the trail to cut a more direct route to the GPS coordinates. I ate a granola bar and consumed a bottle of water and wondered if the deepening cold was imagination or the result of my higher altitude. Trees were fallen and the ground sank in spots, and I had to double back to circumvent a small gorge, moving north and west.

I prided myself that all I needed were four dependent Hobbits and I'd be Aragorn.

Except after another thirty minutes I was lost. I got turned around, unsure which way to face. The sun was directly overhead and providing no help, the rascal. I walked in one direction long enough for the change to register on my iPhone and I altered course, heading back on track. Just like warriors in Middle Earth did.

Tired and getting angry, but nearing the destination, I found a recently used path—two wheel ruts in the dirt. Looked as though trafficked by ATVs. I used my phone to zoom in and around, looking for the path's origin. Might come in from the...west? Used for hunting.

I followed it, enjoying the rocks and hard dirt under my feet instead of wet leaves. The path ran up and around a knoll and there I came to...

37.1612

-80.1716

No wonder Ulysses had marked this place with GPS coordinates. It was nowhere.

Another couple minutes of walking and I saw through

the trees...something. Signs of ancient civilization? I approached and listened and detected no life.

It was a Jeep and the remains of an old wooden building, so hidden they didn't appear on Google Earth. Probably a hunting shed. A fire had eaten most and only one wall still stood. The floors were rotten and yielding to the earth. It'd been erected in a clearing with no foundation other than cinderblocks. No generator, no power lines.

The Jeep Wrangler looked like a model only five years old, but now beyond repair. Animals had burrowed in and torn up the seats and built nests. I opened the driver door and things rustled in the back. The hinges complained. No keys in sight. The glove compartment was open, and resting on top of the user manual I found the faded registration.

This vehicle was registered to...Ulysses Steinbeck.

Zounds.

Eureka.

Elementary.

The inspection ran out three years ago. It'd been sitting here ever since the time of his accident, I bet.

Okay, Ulysses. This place would be hard to find, even following that old ATV trail. But you didn't want to forget it, thus the GPS numbers. You planned on returning. Why?

In the back seat I saw a fiberglass handle. I grabbed and lifted and was holding a shovel in decent shape. I used it to scrape out the car of debris and nests, sending small rodents scampering and releasing a rich odor of life and animal waste. The Jeep was essentially empty.

I kicked around the ruined shed and scrapped soggy boards aside. The wooden fibers parted and fell. Buried underneath old shingles I found a bizarre contraption connected to a battery coated with acid. I sat in a dry spot and poked through the mess of wires and saw...needles? I picked up metal parts and discarded them. What were these, maybe bottles of...ink, maybe? All the labels were gone. Needles and ink and this powered contraption...

I felt confident I'd discovered a tattoo kit. A do-it-yourself machine. I'd bet five bucks a forensic technician could look through this quagmire and locate the remnants of animal tranquilizer. And probably a razor to shave a dog, and some disinfectant.

Ulysses had brought GPS here, knocked her out, shaved her, and tattooed her with the coordinates. That would be a doozy of a journal entry.

I poked through the rest of the remains. Found an old cast-iron pan and a stainless steel mug. Some other stuff I couldn't identify. I walked the perimeter of the ruins and saw nothing. I circled it again looked and thought.

What had I learned?

Ulysses Steinbeck had a secret shed.

But it was nearly impossible to get here. In fact, I bet he'd gotten lost a few times finding it. So he'd come up here with a puppy in the Jeep and a tattoo kit. Once here, he used a GPS device to determine the latitude and longitude and he'd tattooed it onto the side of a dog. Much easier to find now. And he returned home without the Jeep.

To a well-trained and keen eye like mine, it all made sense.

Except not really, no it didn't.

What on *earth*, Ulysses.

I GOT LOST GETTING BACK to my car. Took an hour longer than it should.

This is why Gandalf never asked me to help.

25

Kix and I played with Georgina Princess at the park off Grandin until dusk. GPS reacted with dignity and polite interest at the sight of other dogs, but she much preferred the company of my son and me. We threw a ball and pushed on the swing and slid down slides until we couldn't see one another, and decided hours spent thusly were the reason we existed.

Timothy August made chicken soup with cauliflower instead of noodles. Manny and I ate with him and Stackhouse until he claimed he could do more pushups than me, and we had to quit to determine supremacy. I collapsed at fifty. He stopped at fifty-five, though he could've kept going. I laid on the floor gasping. He hopped up and kept eating.

"It's because," I said. I sounded like someone with a cervix dilated to ten centimeters and pushing. "It's because you're skin and bones. While I'm hauling a lot more muscle around."

Manny ate soup and watched me on the floor. "Hey muscles, you need CPR?"

"I might."

Kix laughed and pointed.

Georgina Princess nuzzled my ear.

That evening I sat on the couch with my laptop and I surfed to Roanoke County's online recorder of deeds, and I zoomed in on the map to Ulysses's GPS coordinates.

One guy owned all that land. Hundreds of acres. Larry Alexander. I Googled him and discovered a Larry Alexander living in Roanoke, using the white pages. The white pages! Online phonebooks still had use, who knew. Glanced at my watch; it was too late to call.

Veronica Summers parked her car and came in after nine. She came straight to my couch, kissed me on the mouth, curled up with her head in my lap and said, "I don't want to talk. I just want to be."

After a minute she rearranged, pulling a throw pillow under her head, still on my lap, and said, "This house. It gets me every time."

She fell asleep soon after, breathtaking in repose.

I rested my arm around her and changed the television to SportsCenter and watched basketball highlights and wondered what during the course of her day had wiped her out and decided it didn't matter because I was willing to spend the rest of my evenings on couches with her, no matter the reasons.

26

Saturday, I took Kix to Wasena park. Georgina Princess joined and so did Ronnie, holding GPS by the leash until we reached a deserted field between the tennis courts and baseball diamond. I threw the tennis ball and she raced for it.

Georgina, not Ronnie.

Kix stumbled after GPS and I threw the ball again when it was returned, and the poor boy never seemed to catch up.

Manny and Beck arrived, stepping out of the super-charged American sports car and wearing marshal gear. Manny ran in a large circle with GPS and I said, "Look at them as they gyre and gimble in the wabe."

Beck wrinkled her nose. "Is that another language?"

"No, philistine. It's poetry."

Soon Manny and Veronica were both kneeling and playing with the dog and Kix. They spoke to her in high-pitched voices and I noted with despair, "They are descending into anarchy."

"You don't like her?" said Beck.

"I do. Far more than I anticipated. But why do they squeak around her?"

"Manny and Veronica? That's how you reward a dog. Look how much she likes it."

"Dogs are rewarded by high-pitched voices?" I said.

"Don't you use a more excited voice when Kix needs a reward?"

"That hypothetical situation hasn't happened yet. He's an abject sinner."

She laughed. Because I'm so funny.

"That's not true. Kix is great," she said. "But the voice might be hard for you. Yours is deeper than most."

I swelled with pride. Yeah it was.

Beck pointed at the dog. "See how she watches you? And runs over here occasionally? She likes you. You're the alpha."

"Because I feed her, probably."

"Maybe. I'm no expert. I just grew up with dogs in the house."

That evening I sat with the dog and petted her, and debated the merits of pet versus petted as the past tense verb, and decided I disliked both. I assumed a falsetto—a manly one, which made it okay—and told her she was a good girl. She opened her mouth and it seemed to be a smile, which was impossible I thought, but the impression remained; she was happy.

IT SNOWED THE NEXT DAY, but lightly, and we went to church. Ronnie accompanied, humoring me. She once said, "Any God who truly loves me needs to have his halo adjusted."

"After reading about him, I find his affection for us to be irresponsible and reckless."

"Like how you feel about Kix."

"Potentially more so."

"I suppose if you're going to believe in some weird religion, you may as well choose the most affectionate deity," said Ronnie.

Though blasphemer, she looked good in a pew. Her dress exposed her shoulders and somehow on her the naked shoulders and neck looked scandalous, and the nearby parishioners had trouble focusing.

Was parishioner correct? I still had no great handle on the lexicon. Member of the congregation? One of the flock?

I sat next to Marcus Morgan. Ronnie sat on the far side, near his wife Courtney so they could whisper.

The rector (pastor? priest? clergy? ecclesiastic?) taught sanctification and the necessary byproducts of suffering. Marcus nodded enthusiastically and called an, "Amen!" which seemed to shock the stoic gathering but please the man at the mic.

After church we all took naps. In bed, under the covers, she murmured into the small of my neck, "That man is insane."

"How so?"

"Suffering is the worst."

"Does it not strengthen us? He claims so."

"My suffering didn't, I don't think. Drove me near to suicide." Her eyes were closed, her hand under my shirt and resting on my abdomen.

"I think what he wanted to say was, even the hard things in life can be redeemed if you find meaning and growth. Holy moments can be found in the dark and scrape away the dross."

"I like that. But does it matter?"

"Maybe. What is life other than a series of moments? Other than the unstoppable sequence of events in which we constantly change? And if we have no choice but to change, it's important to be changing upward instead of downward. And if we take control of every moment, instead of letting it control us, and if we decide the series of moments can be redeemed, even the dark ones, then our life is better," I said, wondering if I should process these things more thoroughly before uttering them out loud.

"Wow. Did that pastor guy say all that? Was that his point?"

"No but it should have been. I don't think he carried his argument far enough to the highest possible conclusions."

She yawned. "Mackenzie."

"Yes Ronnie."

"Sometimes I remember how intelligent you are. How profound and deep, and I realize that you are outthinking everyone else around you. And I get all goosebumpy because you want to be with me."

"Objection, goosebumpy is not a word."

"Um, how about, galvanized? Or indicted?"

"Much better."

"Mackenzie." Very soft now.

"Yes Ronnie."

"Moments like this are holy for me. Or as close as I'll ever get."

In the next room, Kix shouted at GPS and threw toys.

"Dog. Fish! Fish dog."

Georgina Princess patiently fetched the toys, raised up to place her front paws on the rim of the pack 'n play and dropped the toys back in, and Kix did it again and again until he grew sleepy and we were content.

27

I called Larry Alexander. From the sound of it, Larry was maybe eighty-five and attached to an oxygen machine.

"Sorry to bother you, Mr. Alexander. I happened to be hiking through the woods and got lost and ended up on your property recently on top of Bent Mountain."

The voice on the other end made a chuckling sound. "Oh. That's okay. Mighty fine of you to let me know, but...oh, I got so much land that I don't know what to do with. Expect I'll give it to my son and he won't know either." He chuckled some more.

"I noticed a burned down shed and old Jeep, not far from a trail I used. Any idea the story?"

"Yeah, I do...let's see, maybe I can...maybe I can remember." There were some scratching sounds. "Yeah, I do, so...a friend of mine, no, that's not it...my nephew uses the land to hunt. Fine with me. And he's got, what do you call them, lodges maybe, scattered about. Few years back, a friend of mine asked if he could make use of one, and he went up there in the Jeep, but...as I recall he got into an automobile crash, and...well, the

Jeep's still there. And, oh let's see, I heard about a year later from my nephew, his name's Shannon, Shannon told me the shed burned down but the Jeep survived, so...I guess it'll just set there and rot until the end of time." More chuckling.

"These things happen, I guess."

"Yes, I guess they do," said Larry.

"What was your friend doing in the Jeep up at the shed? Hunting, I suppose?"

"No, don't think so. He was a, well, a learned man who didn't care to hunt. I expect he just liked to get away. You know? Get out of the city now and then."

"I know the feeling."

"Poor man, not sure what happened to him after the accident."

That's funny, Larry Alexander, because I'm not sure what happened to him *before* it.

I HAD QUESTIONS.

I needed answers.

Ulysses wouldn't have them. He couldn't remember them, after all. But it was his door I knocked upon later that day.

Rose let me in, looking pleased to see me. As always, she was barefoot.

"Perfect timing, Mr. August. He woke from a nap an hour ago."

I paused in the foyer. "Rose, I am confused about something. You were the housekeeper, right?"

"I was. Before the accident." she said. "I still am, I suppose."

"And then the ex-wife and daughter asked you to move in and provide full-time care."

"Yes."

"Why you? Don't take it personally, but I wouldn't think to ask a housekeeping professional to provide medical attention."

"Ah. Yes." She smiled and placed her hand on my arm for a brief moment. Probably to verify bicep circumference and brag to her friends. "I see your confusion, Mr. August. I am a certified nurse. I used to work part-time with hospice, and while at homes I cleaned when I grew bored and the nicer families would tip me for the service. Word spread enough so that I was doing both jobs."

"Ah hah."

"You see?"

"I do."

"Mr. Steinbeck and his ex-wife offered to pay me better than I was making before at both. His insurance helps, of course. It's enough to help my son through college."

"I didn't know you had one."

"Yes, Jason." She smiled the biggest smile I'd seen yet. "He's at UVA. He is my joy."

She led me to the office where Ulysses Steinbeck sat at a chair near the fire reading a book. "Ulysses? Mackenzie August to see you." She took three journals from his desk and placed them on his chair's side table.

Ulysses stood and shook my hand, and smiled politely and without recognition. He glanced at the two whiteboards in the room, read the information, and said, "Thank you, Rose."

She left.

He indicated the journals. "Before we speak, Mr. August, I need to refresh my memory."

I sat in the opposite chair. "I know the drill, Dr. Steinbeck. Happy to wait and enjoy your fire until you're ready."

"I recognize your cologne."

"The reason I wore it."

"Very helpful." He glanced in *What Is Happening Now* and noted I wasn't scheduled. He muttered my name a few times and flipped backwards in the journal, scanning each page. He spoke softly to himself and I couldn't make out the words. He found me from last week and said, "Ah. Ah hah, yes. Okay. Good, good. Mr. August, yes, nice to see you again. You're finding the dog."

"I'm here to update you and seek counsel."

He smiled the smile of a man still catching up. "By all means. I'm hazy on the details but I know I'm eager for news about the dog."

"We have a weird situation here, Dr. Steinbeck, because it's almost like I have two clients."

"Explain."

"You hired me to find the dog. But you don't know why. You're hoping the reason becomes apparent and when it does you're hoping I'll know what to do."

He nodded. "My notes say you are trustworthy."

"It's a little like you hired me to help your past self. Because your past self knew things you currently don't. But your past self has no agency here, other than me. And your current self doesn't know the answers. And now I know some of them, and you're hoping the right thing will be done, even if you don't know what it is and even though you can't really control things. Make sense?"

He had been scratching notes in his journal. He paused and considered me. "I often experience this dilemma. It's a helpless and frustrating sensation."

"Considering your plight and the fact that I have control right now, I want you to know I'm doing my best."

"You have control."

"Yes, organic but not permanent."

He made a humming noise. Looked at his notes. Looked at the board again. Sighed with displeasure. "You're asking for more money."

"No."

"Then..."

"I've been paid and paid well. I'm not here to extort you."

"Okay." He fidgeted in the chair, waiting for the other shoe to drop. Dropped the journal with a thump and bent to retrieve it.

"I need more information and we need to make a decision."

"One second." He wrote again in his journal. He got lost, read from a few pages ago, scanned his notes again from today, and wrote some more. Pronounced, "I'm ready."

"I found the dog. I have the dog. I discovered a secret the dog was keeping."

His pen paused. "That's satisfying news. Right?"

"Not yet. I can tell you what I know but you'll be *dis*satisfied. I don't have all the answers yet and I think that's ultimately what you're after. But...you need to decide if you want me to continue."

"Why wouldn't I?"

"The weeks leading up to the divorce finalization, you acted out of character. Aggressively so. And you're essentially asking me to go digging into that time period. You need to decide if you want that man's secrets unearthed."

"I had secrets."

"At least one." The paramour.

"So it's not just about the dog."

"Georgina Princess is merely the tip of the iceberg, I think."

"Georgina Princess." His face paled. "That...that tugs at me. You know, sometimes I almost remember it."

"Her."

Ulysses didn't hear. He smiled sadly. "Alex always wanted a dog." He made some slow scratches on the paper. "Do you have guesses about things you might discover?"

"I have guesses. But I don't want to tell you yet."

"Is money involved?"

"I suspect so. But maybe don't write that down."

"Hmm." He stood and stared at the fire. He kept talking to himself under his breath, probably to keep things fresh in his mind. He paced the room, glancing again and again at the whiteboards. Sat back down and read in his journal. "This is a lot to absorb and I'm not sure how to do it. Or how to proceed or what to say."

"Understood. It comes down to this. I can quit now and give you the simple answers and it might bring you peace. Or I can keep going and get the truth."

"If...if the truth you uncover implicates my 'past self' in some sort of crime, are you obligated to alert the authorities?" He spoke the words slowly, like trying to pull them out from fog.

"No. And I won't."

"Are you obligated to tell anyone else?"

"No. And you'll need to trust my discretion and my promise that I have the best interest of you and your family in mind."

He stared at his journal for a long time, resting his cheek in his hand. Big sigh. "I need the truth. I want to know."

"Okay."

"But, dammit, I have no idea how to document this." He

wiped at his eyes and sniffed, and he was dealing with emotion hitherto I hadn't noticed. I sat patiently and soon his pen began scratching.

He wrote, *Trust Mackenzie. He's still working at the truth. He has the best interest of you and Alex at heart.*

For reasons I couldn't immediately identify, his words went straight into my inner recesses and suddenly I was dealing with emotions hitherto unexpected.

I wondered why he wrote Alex's name. Habit? Subconscious slip?

I cleared my throat. "Did you ever like to get away, Dr. Steinbeck? Before the accident. Escape to nature to clear your mind? Cabin in the woods, maybe?"

He sniffed. "I wish. Too late now."

Rose came in, carrying a tray. She said, "Mind if I eavesdrop a moment? I have coffee and tea."

Ulysses straightened and wiped more at his eyes and set his pen down. "Yes of course, Rose. Thank you. I can't quite remember why I'm so damn emotional at the moment."

28

A dim realization hit me the following morning as I drank coffee and watched Ronnie leave in her Mercedes for the office. The topic of our future still felt nuclear, too hot to touch directly and we danced around it, enjoying each moment like there wouldn't be another, but with looming dread. As our bonds deepened, the stakes raised, and Ronnie wobbled like an amateur poker player suddenly betting with big money. She'd never cared about tomorrow until she was with me and she worried she would ruin it all. Suffering anxiety about future events which would probably never happen.

Kix and I watched her from the door and she blew kisses from her car as she left.

My first car, father? A red Mercedes and I'll accept nothing less, said Kix and he laughed at Georgina Princess.

A strange thought, my son driving one day—leaving in my car and me having nothing to drive, being stuck at home.

Stuck at home.

"Huh," I said to myself. "How about that."

Okay, fine. I'll take a Lexus, if I must.

Light bulbs flashing between my ears. "The Jeep, Kix. That's the answer. The Jeep and the Audi."

Yes yes. Either will do, sure. Maybe I'm not as picky as I thought. But I'd still prefer the Mercedes, Pops.

I DROVE to Virginia Tech and parked near Owens Dining Hall. The wind blew harder here today than in Roanoke but temperatures were above freezing and I wasn't forced to reevaluate my life choices, and that was nice.

I called Alex. She answered brightly and I said, "I'll be driving near Blacksburg soon. Can I buy you a coffee and update you about the dog and get your thoughts on something?"

"Absolutely, Mr. August. Is my father okay?"

"He's dynamite. Saw him yesterday."

"Any reason we can't talk now over the phone? I've got time."

Argh. Think fast, Mackenzie. "I gotta take another call in a minute, so I can't. Meet you at Owens Dining Hall later today? Pick a time."

"Does thirty minutes work? Or an hour?"

"Yes. I'll be there in thirty minutes."

"Where are you now?"

Argh. Think faster, Mackenzie. "Interstate 81, heading...north."

"See you then!" and she hung up.

I enjoyed the youth and their energy. Very little of my daily interactions could be described as vibrant exclamations.

Twenty-five minutes later I spotted her trotting across

the street and into Owens. I waited three minutes and followed her in.

She waved to me from a line and dramatically pointed at a table where I should wait, amidst a sea of other youths. I obeyed and got a thumbs up from her and askew glances from kids who looked vaguely like her but less shiny.

She returned with two coffees and two boxes of Chick-fil-A nuggets and she gave me half. I remarked, "It is not you who should be supplying the food."

"You're helping my dad, and each semester I have meals going to waste, so..." She shrugged.

She looked bright and sparkly, as though at any moment she might take a selfie for Instagram and get ten thousand hearts or likes or favorites or whatever the hell they were.

We ate and drank some and I said, "I found Georgina Princess Steinbeck and I'm now her owner. More or less."

"Oh good! Does Dad know?"

"Yes. Or he did, temporarily. Part of the reason why I'm currently her owner is that he doesn't want to be."

She laughed and quickly squeezed my wrist. "I figured. Does this put the issue to rest? In his mind? I hope so."

"Not yet. I'd like to talk to you about the ongoing questions."

"Okay. Absolutely I want to help." She nodded, less eager though.

"Three things to discuss." I held up three fingers—my pinky, ring, and middle fingers. "The first thing I know. The second thing, I got a guess. The third, I'm clueless."

She ate a nugget and looked a little nervous.

I said, "First, I know you were at the crash. Presumably you were in the car when it went off the road. You used a fake name, but you were there. I spoke to the officer. No biggie—you panicked. I'm not sharing that with anyone."

She didn't respond but gazed into her coffee. Her face lost some color the same way her father's did. If I'd mentioned this over the phone, she might deny it; lying is harder face-to-face.

I said, "It's been bugging me—*why* were you there? Whatever the reason, it was worth lying to the police. And then I found the shed in the woods with your father's Jeep."

Her breath caught and the surface of the coffee in her cup trembled. "You know about that place?"

"I do."

"How?"

"I do this for a living. I snoop and learn. The Jeep is still up there."

She nodded.

I said, "The Jeep helped me divine the reason you were in the wrecked Audi that night. That, and a photograph I saw at your father's house."

"Which photograph?"

"The photograph of you getting your first car. Know the one? In the kitchen on the wall?"

She nodded.

"You smiling with the Audi, with the big red bow."

She nodded more.

"So this is the second thing, Alex. I don't know for sure, but I have a guess. You were driving the night of the accident. Ulysses didn't drive off the road—you did. The Audi was registered to him but it was your car. That's why the Jeep is still up there, because it had to be left—"

She stood suddenly. "I don't..." She walked away. Not a storm off but close. I waited. She got near the exit and paused. Some students went around her and gave her second looks. After a minute she moved to a nearby table and sat. Her shoulders hunched and her head bowed and she cried. Twenty-five feet away from me.

Mackenzie August, you charmer, you.

I waited five minutes while she cried and sniffed and blew her nose in a napkin. Her friends saw her and checked, and they talked and then her friends left.

She looked at her phone. Scrolled the screen a while. Stood and came back.

Her face looked swollen and blotchy and she said, "So? So what. So I was driving."

"*So* you feel responsible, even though you aren't. *So* it'll eat at you the rest of your life, Alex. I know how these things work. You wake up remembering it. You blame yourself. You hate yourself. You want to forget and you can't, and the worst part is you can't tell anyone. I bet I'm the first."

She hugged her elbows. "My father isn't paying you to bolster my mental well-being."

"That's free of charge. Because I like him. And I like you."

She sat, laid her head down and made a sobbing sound into the surface of the table.

"The Jeep is still up there because you came to pick him up. In your Audi. Him and the mysterious woman."

She didn't move her head.

I said, "It's not your fault, Alex."

"Yes. Yes it is."

"No. It's not. I can prove it. Your dad called you because he'd gotten drunk and set fire to the shed and badly burned himself. Right?"

She raised up. Reached for napkins to wipe her eyes and mop the pool of tears she'd left on the table. "Jeez, Mr. August. How do you know all this? All this awful shit I thought was long gone."

"Rose told me a nurse tended your father's burn wounds. But I saw the pictures and the Audi hadn't caught fire when it crashed. So why was he burned? Then I saw the shed. He'd burned himself. I'm amazed you found that shed at night and that your Audi made it up the trail."

"It didn't." She half-laughed. "They couldn't drive because..." A pause to blow her nose. "You're right, they got drunk. Knocked over a candle or lantern or something. My father never drank but he...he was blasted. Alcohol poisoning, I think." All her words sounded funny, her nose too congested to articulate.

Blood alcohol content that high can lead to amnesia, especially combined with additional head trauma.

I said, "How'd you find the place?"

"Somehow she had the GPS coordinates for the shed. She was drunk too, *really* drunk. A miracle she figured out how to find the longitude and latitude. The Audi got close but couldn't get over a ridge. I had to help carry him half a mile."

I didn't tell her, but it wasn't a miracle—Ulysses had been up there before with the express purpose of nailing the GPS coordinates. And then tattooing them on a puppy.

I said, "The women, his girlfriend?"

"I guess. Sure. At the time."

"He was in bad shape."

She nodded, looking at the tissue and sniffing. "Awful."

"The alcohol and the burns."

"Yes."

"And you were shaken and racing to the hospital and lost control of the Audi around the tight turns coming down Bent Mountain."

The structure of her face crumbled again and her lip quivered and she nodded more. "I nearly crashed at the top.

I swiped a guardrail. He was blitzed and throwing up, and he said, 'If we crash, tell them I was driving. Okay Alex?' He kept saying my name over and over. 'Okay, Alex? Alex? Right?' And then he'd throw up more. And when we *did* crash...the woman insisted. She said, 'Tell them your dad was driving so you don't get in trouble.' And when the police arrived, that's what she said. So..."

"Don't you see, Alex? Not your fault. They needed a hospital but they called you, not an ambulance. It's impossible to drive well when your father is dying in the passenger seat. You had to shoulder the burden of other people's foolish mistakes."

She reclined in the chair, dropped her head back, and closed her eyes. "That was a bad night. I tried to forget it."

I said, "You gotta talk to someone about this. The weight crushes you."

"Like counseling? I don't want to. Can't afford it."

"You trust your mom enough to talk with her? She doesn't know the truth, I don't think."

"She doesn't. But she's with Gordon now. And I hate that guy. We all do." She erected herself and cleared the tissues and took them to the trash. Returned and got another and blew her nose again but it didn't help. Gave me a wry smile. "You want to know who the mysterious woman is. That's the third thing you want to talk about."

"Yes."

"I'm not telling and I think you should let that part go. Dad doesn't even remember her, and it wouldn't help anything if you find out."

"It might."

"Mr. August, this whole thing is so sad. Right? It's awful. What good is this doing?"

"It's the truth."

"So?"

"The truth has a way of freeing us."

"Doesn't feel like it. Are you going to tell anyone? That I was driving?"

"Of course not. You suffered enough. But I think you should. Someone you can trust," I said.

"I don't have a boyfriend."

"You could tell your mother."

"She's better at pretending than you think. We get along, but... I don't know, it's complicated. When they split, I stayed with Dad and she...she wanted money in child support and it hurt our relationship."

"Money has a way of doing that," I said.

"So are you done? Can you leave this thing alone now?"

"I'll leave you alone. I promise."

"What else is there?"

"An excellent question," I said.

"You're going to find out. You're good at this, I can tell."

At the moment, watching her dab her eyes and sniff, I didn't feel like it.

29

I had most of the puzzle finished. Over fifty percent. And the remainder was constituted by only two pieces.

Who was the woman?

Why tattoo the dog?

I had guesses about both.

Other than making beautiful young girls cry, I was having a ton of fun. I preferred this to cage matches in Naples.

I waited in the woods behind Robin Hood, on a path leading to the Mill Mountain Star, and I watched Ulysses's house at a distance of fifty yards. Temperatures fell into the forties and I shivered and stamped and waited for Rose to go somewhere.

Less fun.

Finally, about three in the afternoon, the garage door purred open and an old Mercedes A-Class backed out. Rose at the wheel. She motored down Robin Hood and out of sight. I waited ten minutes and knocked on his door.

I wore cologne. But a starkly different brand and scent. Less musk, more fruit.

Ulysses himself answered it. Wearing loafers and a black turtleneck and corduroy khakis.

"Afternoon," I said.

He nodded politely. There was no flicker of recognition in his eyes—I was a stranger. Fascinating. "Good afternoon. Help you?"

I wore the blue shirt of a handyman and I indicated the bag of tools I carried. "Sorry I'm late, Dr. Steinbeck. Here to check the thermostat. Heater's acting funny, Rose said. She mentioned you wouldn't remember I'm coming."

He nodded the nod of a man resigned to memory loss but not entirely crushed by it. "I forgot she called you."

"I'll only be ten minutes and Rose said to let myself out. Sound good?"

"She's the boss," said Ulysses and he stepped aside. "Thermostat's in the kitchen. If you need me, I'll be in my office."

"Perfect. Thanks, Doc," I said.

Robbing this man would be hilariously easy. Should warn Rose.

I deposited my bag down in the gourmet kitchen, salivated over the Wusthof knives, debated cooking a five course meal, decided against it, and moved into the living quarters beyond. Found a main hallway and staircase. My guess— they didn't live upstairs; they took up residence on the main floor so there I searched.

Rose's bedroom was first. An open J.D. Robb novel rested on the nightstand, face down. Bed made. Laundry put away. A vase on the dresser with flowers three days past bloom. Two framed photographs with her son. Phone charging station. Thin necklaces hanging on the mirror.

The bathroom Rose used was the bathroom across the hall. The usual stuff—a brush clogged with her long brown

hair; shower with assortment of shampoos and condition-
ers; contact solution; hair dryer; a pill box. I could invade
her privacy and inspect her prescriptions but that wasn't
why I came.

I moved on.

Ulysses's bedroom was the master. Still orderly but less
so. I found what I wanted immediately—notes on the wall
for him to see as soon as he woke each morning. The largest
was a decorative oil painting dominated by a sweet
message—

Good morning, Ulysses.
The most important things for you to know are this:
Your family loves you.
You are not in debt. No one is mad at you.
Your health is good. Your daughter is happy.
Your schedule is clear. Your friends might drop by.
And you have memory loss.
You read this yesterday too, but you forgot already.
You're going to be okay. Take a moment to breathe.
And don't panic—today will be a good day.

This annotated oil painting was framed and remained
on the wall permanently. Large and prominent. Below the
note about not panicking were functional suggestions about
the best way for him to cope with this fresh news and get
started with the day.

Jeez. I scrubbed at my hair, battling intense but brief
claustrophobia. Imagine waking up to that every. single. day.
Each morning a dizzying sensation as you read the news for
the first time. Again.

Now that I thought about it, he might need to read this
painting several times during a twenty-four-hour period.
Wow.

A little whiteboard hung adjacent, on which Rose wrote

notes. For example, she was grocery shopping at three and would be back by four-thirty.

Below that, another painting. Framed but smaller. This one had less dust on it, probably because it was taken off the wall occasionally, due to company.

My dearest Ulysses,

You and I are in love. Sometimes you remember this but usually you do not, and that's okay. The gap in your memory begins a few weeks before you proposed.

You remember me most often as Rose, the house-keeper, a woman you love in secret.

But in reality, between us there are no secrets. I am the woman who adores you most in the whole world. And you loved me before the car crash you've forgotten.

We will never get married.

But we will be together forever.

Come find me in the house! I look forward to seeing you every day.

I love you. Always.

Rose.

A Polaroid was taped to the frame, the two of them kissing. She wore an engagement ring. Looking younger and carefree.

The impact knocked my knees out. I sat heavily onto the floor. She was the mysterious woman, obviously.

I should have known. And I had on some level.

But I had NOT known that Ulysses had proposed.

He'd proposed, but then the accident, and...

And she stayed. She stayed with a man who didn't remember he loved her.

For half an hour I couldn't find the strength to get up.

∾

I SAT in my car later that day. Unable to turn the ignition, still numb from the evidence of unconditional love in the face of constant pain. Rose Bridges, my new hero.

My phone rang. Marcus Morgan calling.

I shook myself free of reverie. One does not ignore calls from the local cocaine lord.

I put it on speaker.

He said, "Got a call from Tom. You remember Tom."

"Tom Garrett. One of the Kings, looks like Mr. Rogers, runs identify fraud. Big fan of mine."

"That he is. Got a call from Tom. He did a little digging into the, ah, windfall from your gladiatorial endeavors."

"I won the Gabbia Cremisi in Naples and now I'm rich."

"You half right. But fuckers say they keeping your winnings," he said.

"I'm not surprised."

"No?"

"I broke out of their cage and killed their guards and burned down their billion dollar hotel."

"Manny the Marshal burned it, matter fact. He set the fires. I know cause I was there and I wasn't in no damn cage."

"Maybe so but I'm taking credit. No one hit him; they all hit me," I said.

"This ain't a world of legal recourse or justice. They say they keeping it, they keep it. Their eyes, you broke the deal."

I snorted. "The deal."

"A gentleman's world running on deals and relationships. Only problem, the gentlemen be gangsters."

"Your first book, Marcus, should be titled *The Gentlemen Be Gangsters*."

"I'll keep that in mind."

"So if I want my money—"

"Hafta go take it. Kill 'em all. Might start a war with the whole damn Camorra," he said.

"Nah. I like what I do and I'm dating an attorney."

"Thought you might let it go. Ain't yo style."

"You killed What's-his-name, so who's running the show in Naples now?"

"Don't know, don't care."

"Well, tell Tom they can keep the money long as they build a museum for children and erect a statue of me out front."

"Yeah. Fo'sure I'll tell him that."

"Out of curiosity, if I demanded my money and started a war with the Camorra, would the Kings back me up?"

He sighed loud enough for the receiver to distort the sound. Took another moment before answering. "A good damn question, August. Winning the tournament? That's a big deal. Made the Kings proud. Now the council running the thing slights you, means they slight the Kings too. You as famous as The Prince, remember him? But, be that as it may...you ain't exactly the Kings' golden son. So...I don't know, August."

"I'm not gonna push the issue."

"One more thing. The sale of Veronica Summers's property is finalized. I already got a handle of the wholesaler issue. But it's creating waves with specific individuals."

"Like Darren Robbins? And the men who love Ronnie? And the men who fear us both?"

"Who else. Think they gonna go away quietly? Cause they ain't. Just letting you know. You got this weird status among people who matter. Half of them love you, cause of the tournament. Other half? Well...let's just say, I still got an ear to the ground. Cause the issue is ongoing."

"Understood. And I appreciate it."

"No thanks needed. Couple of us made a small fortune betting on you."

"How nice," I said.

"We got wealth, you got a free tattoo."

"Wasn't exactly free. But Ronnie likes the design."

"All that matters."

I was in my car, within sight of Ulysses's house. And Rose's house.

I said, "Yeah. You're right."

30

Ronnie and Kix came home at six as I was feeding Georgina Princess. Ronnie had taken the afternoon off, collected Kix, and spent several hours in a whirlwind downtown—Kids Square, boutique shopping, transportation museum, food and treats, more boutiques, more food and treats. Kix toddled my way, unsteady steps, huge smile, not far from an insulin coma.

I collected him and wiped his face.

Ronnie kissed me and went for white wine. We weren't on bad terms. We were on weird terms. Two oxen, yoked together and realizing the other traveled at a differing speed.

Miles Davis played on the speakers and the heat was set at seventy-one to keep out the January chill.

I said, "Good afternoon?"

"The best, Mackenzie. The *best*. Kix and I are Bonnie and Clyde, and I love him to death. He had a milkshake and a hotdog and cookies and ice cream, and I got some pashmina."

"You're spoiling him. Professional boxers are never spoiled as children."

"Boxer? Ick. One day he'll take over my practice, the handsomest attorney in Virginia."

"And the fattest?" I said.

"It'll add to his boyish charm."

Kix ignored us, eyes on Georgina Princess. I set him in his playpen where he wobbled sleepily.

Ronnie said, "Don't feed me. I'm stuffed. On the way here, guess who called?"

"Ruth Bader Ginsburg. She needs you to take her seat on the bench."

"No, but I debate getting a RBG tattoo. Lynsey called."

"Who?"

"Lynsey. No D. The prostitute."

"Elton the felon's girl."

Ronnie lowered onto the kitchen stool and sipped wine. "She said Elton hasn't hit her the last few days. And even told her to take a day off."

"Well, well." I got my bottle of beer off the counter and toasted her. "Look at us, forming a more perfect union and establishing justice and ensuring domestic tranquility."

She clinked my glass. "Are you quoting the Constitution?"

"Botching it."

"But really, Mackenzie. This burns inside me. The need to protect these girls. And I think we can do it. Men like Elton need rules and direction and consequences. So do the girls. Plus safety and counseling, and...that's what I'm using the money for."

"You haven't spent it all?"

She poked me. I liked it. "I gave the money to my finance guy. First I opened up retirement accounts for each of us. Hefty ones. And I kept some more cash. But still, there's over a million and a half being put into a fund I'll use to build the shelter."

"When you say shelter, do you mean brothel?"

"Of course not," said Ronnie. "Maybe. I should ask my counselor about the idea."

"That poor woman, you're going to kill her."

"You don't like the idea of a brothel, I can tell."

I drank some beer and codified my thoughts. "You recognize the reality that prostitution is here to stay. It's better to deal with reality than fantasy. And I like your instincts to protect the girls. But you becoming a madam? I don't like the idea."

"I'd be the madam with the best legs."

"You'd be great. You're a wounded healer. But I'd rather not visit your legs behind bars."

"You break the law all the time, Mackenzie. For the greater good, I realize. Why can't I?"

"My crimes are minor. And though I know you have the best intentions at heart, the prosecutors will book you for sex trafficking. Not minor."

"Maybe I should stick with being a defense attorney?" she said. She finished the glass of wine and crossed her legs. "Let's change the subject. I've been waiting all day to hear about yours. Last I heard, you suspected Alex might have been driving her father's car when it crashed."

"She was in fact."

"I *knew* it."

"You're good at this."

She said, "The saga continues. Did you make her cry?"

"Not intentionally."

"Mackenzie."

I never loved my name so much as when uttered

between those lips. I said, "It was a bad night. All I did was jog her memory."

"Poor kid, she was in a rough spot."

"Some fathers ask too much of their daughters," I said.

"Don't I know. What else?"

"The mysterious woman at the crash? His caretaker. Rose. No big surprise there, probably should've guessed. But the current circumstances will make your hat fly off. Ulysses proposed to her before the accident. Probably within a few days of it."

Ronnie gasped. Her hand went to her mouth like a pinup girl, eyes round. "He can't remember, can he?"

"He cannot."

"Ho. Ly. Shit. How does that work? It's not like they can get married. Right? He'd forget it every morning. He'd forget the wedding a few hours before it began."

"It'd be close to impossible."

"That's horrible. So...she just...what? She stays and works? And hopes?"

I said, "I haven't spoken with her about it yet. I think they daily exist in a state of romantic nascence. Not a bad place to be, but there's no deepening resonance."

"Because daily he has to remember he's not still married to What's-her-face."

"In his mind, he's still married to Colleen. He constantly expects the divorce to be finalized soon. Even though it was several years ago."

"And Rose, how does she manage?"

"I don't know."

"She just...loves him," said Ronnie. "That's, I—I don't have words. Loves, like the verb. She just *does* it?"

"Without ever getting back enough affection or appreciation in return."

Ronnie stood. Took her wine glass to the sink and walked to the door. Slipped out of her shoes. Her eyes were far away.

Georgina Princess watched her from her spot on the rug. Watched her without moving her head.

Ronnie said, "Is it romantic or is it hell? I can't decide. But I'd watch a cheesy movie about it."

"I'd read a Grisham book and hold your hand while you did."

"So is the case closed?"

"Almost. A final detail to confirm and then I present Ulysses with my results."

Ronnie bent at the waist to get her hands on Kix. She lofted him from the pen and onto her shoulder. He'd fallen asleep. Probably wake up in the middle of the night with a stomach ache.

"I'll put him to bed."

I said, "Thanks."

"Not needed. I claim partial ownership." She paused on the second step. "They never exchanged wedding vows. Ulysses and Rose."

"In sickness and in health?"

"But she stays. And cares for him."

"So far."

"You're right," she said and resumed her ascension. "That's enough to make my hat fly off. Whatever the hell that means."

I finished my beer. Tossed it into recycling. Put away her wine glass. Sat on the rug next to Georgina Princess and scratched her near the ears.

My phone rang and I checked it.

Made a hmmmm sound.

How about that. Coincidence?

I let it ring, considering the caller ID and formulating a plan. The best place. A plan worthy of Sherlock Holmes himself.

I answered. "Mackenzie."

"Mr. August? I hope you don't mind the phone call. This is Colleen Gibbs? Do you remember? I was married to Ulysses."

"Of course. Currently you're married to my pal Gordon."

"I am."

"You made me coffee in your kitchen"

She laughed. Maybe a little too hard. "I did. And we talked in your car afterward."

"How can I be of service?"

"Do you have time to meet with me? Tonight? If it's too late for you, tomorrow in your office. I need advice. My daughter called and asked if we could talk; she *never* does this, and I'm curious if it's related to your investigation."

Wheels turning. Plans altering. Winds shifting.

"Um," I said.

"Please."

"I can't tomorrow."

"Oh. I'd like to see you soon."

"Let me update you now on the phone about the investigation." I closed my eyes. Winced, brainstorming. Smoke about to come out ears. Might work. I kept talking but I removed the phone from my ear and opened up a map on screen. "So Gordon was right. The dog, Georgina Princess, is worth a lot of money. A fortune."

Colleen caught her breath. "You're kidding. A fortune? How so?"

"Hard to explain. There's..." I zoomed in on the map and waited for it to refresh. "...there's a house. Near the crash sight. I'm going there tomorrow. Afterwards I'll have more specifics."

"Did you say fortune? I don't understand."

"I don't fully either." If this plan didn't work, I'd hate myself. The image on screen snapped into focus. "But tomorrow morning I should have the money."

"The money? You'll have it? I'm so confused, Mr. August."

"I'm getting it tomorrow. Morning."

"At the house? Where is it? And who owns it?"

"Near Ulysses's crash site. Bottom of Bent Mountain. On..." I squinted at my phone. "On Whistler Drive, off 696."

She said, "Wow. Whistler? Never heard of... Where did the money come from? How does the dog...I'm lost."

"Me too," I said honestly.

"But—"

"One last thing, Colleen?"

"Yes?"

"Remember, Alex is a kid whose entire world crumbled in a matter of months. It's important not to blame her for the mistakes of her parents."

"I'm sorry? Are you—"

I hung up.

31

Georgina Princess and I rented a truck from Enterprise and headed toward Bent Mountain. She rode in the passenger seat, watching me. Her ears were short but not clipped and they flopped forward; reminded me of a girl's pigtails. A thin sliver of white hair started at her nose and ran up between her large brown eyes. Though happy, her forehead wrinkled with concern.

Once this is over, what will happen to me?

I scratched her under the chin. "Once this is over, what would you like to happen?"

I will be happy anywhere.

"Are you happy with us?"

Yes, oh yes.

"Were you happy with Ramona and Ronald Cohen?"

Yes I was.

"Do you think you might be the best dog in the world?"

Yes, oh yes, I am, you'll see.

"You don't really shed. I mean, you do some. But the hairs are so short, and Timothy hasn't complained once."

I am low maintenance and loving and obedient, and I love heating vents and also Kix and also Timothy.

"The problem, Georgina Princess, is that the house is empty most of the day. You'd be bored."

Oh I will protect the house. You will see.

We went south and west. Into the country and I watched my rearview.

No yellow Hummer.

If this didn't work, I was a huge ass.

The day looked colder than it was. The farther into the county we drove, the more fog we encountered and I kept the wipers on low and the defroster pumping. We reached the base of the mountain and turned off on 696—a small road twisting through fields and trees under the watch of looming peaks. The trees were bare and the grass dormant and yellow.

A quarter mile up the road, I passed a private trail. After I passed, a bronze Ford Ranger rumbled out from the private trail and tailed me at an innocuous distance.

"Ah hah!" I told Georgina Princess. "I knew it. This is going to work. See those dummies behind us? They are dummies. My instincts were right. Tell your friends."

Yes, oh yes I will.

We kept going.

An abandoned farmhouse sat lonely and pitiful off Whistler, near the foothills. Once grand, now forgotten and leaning inward. The surrounding fields were wild from neglect—the grass long and brown and choked with dead wildflowers. I rumbled up the pocked gravel drive. A herd of deer, shaggy with winter coats, inspected my ruckus with irritation. I braked near the porch and climbed out, GPS on leash.

The trailing Ford Ranger gave up its innocent pretense

and gunned the engine. The deer bolted, tails raised and flashing white—they executed a series of graceful jumps and vanished into the bracken. The Ranger mashed brakes and slid to a stop, shoveling gravel piles under each tire.

Gordon Gibbs unloaded himself from the passenger seat. He held a pistol—looked like maybe a SIG Sauer 9, a cooler gun than he had any right to. He gripped it awkwardly, like a sword, the dangerous end pointed at me; he was wary of firing it, unsure what would happen.

"What's up, asshole," he said. He wore white Nikes, black track pants, and a long sleeve shirt that said Flag Nor Fail. Blue veins bulged in his neck.

The driver came around the truck. Another beefcake. His head was shaved, but other than that he and Gordon looked eerily similar. Even blue veins in the same spots. Instead of a gun he carried a bat.

Yikes.

Georgina Princess growled.

I said, "Hey look, Gordo. She's a good judge of character. You can't teach that. That's superior breeding, is all."

"You found money, huh? Nice work, gumshoe. Guess what happens now? You'll give it to me."

"I will?"

"Hell yeah you will."

"Why?" I said.

"First, because I'm stronger than you and I can take it by force. How's that for why? Second, it belongs to me legally."

"In fact it does not."

Gordon's friend—upon closer inspection he was more tan, an orange color from a bottle I thought—smacked the barrel of his bat against his palm.

Gordon said, "I married Colleen, asshole. By law it's mine."

"Honestly, Gordon. Find a new insult. Surely you can't be both exceptionally ugly *and* dull? That's a rough go."

"The money's in the house?"

"Not telling."

His buddy, Mr. Tan, chuckled—supposed to be sinister, maybe, or he thought I was hilarious.

Probably the latter.

Gordon grinned. "Yeah. You are telling."

"Nuh uh," I said.

"You're gonna tell me or I shoot the dog. Then we pulp you with the bat."

"Shoot the dog? I'd prefer you didn't. As it happens, I've grown fond of her. Can you believe it?"

"I don't give a shit, August. Take us there."

"Colleen told you about the money," I said.

Georgina Princess had placed herself between me and them. She strained against the leash, nose to the ground. She was growling, but I felt it through the leash more than I heard it.

"Don't matter how I know about the money."

"Colleen's the only person other than me who knew," I said. "So...Colleen told you. Not a lot of options."

"Don't matter."

"It does to me. I'm disappointed in Colleen. I liked her. She touched my arm several times."

"She what?"

"I liked it, up until this minute. Does she still touch your arm?"

"Screw you, August. The money belongs to her, so shove your disappointment where the sun don't shine. Now where is it?"

"The disappointment? Or the place where the sun doesn't shine? Because—"

"Shut up! Jee-zus, what a pain you are," he shouted.

"Oh. You mean the money?"

"Where is it?"

Mr. Tan said, "Gibbs, I'll hit him with the bat. Couple times, and we'll see if he's still so funny."

"I will be. It's instinctual."

"August. I'm about to kill your dog."

"You can't hit her," I said.

"Think you can stop me?"

"I didn't mean, *I won't let you.* I mean, you can't. You'll miss."

"The hell I will."

"I'm not convinced you know where the trigger is," I said.

Mr. Tan took a step closer. He waggled the bat near GPS, a casual and mean motion. "Think I'll miss with this? I'll beat the teeth out of your dog. And then you. Get me?"

"You guys work out together? What do you bench?" I said.

"I bench—"

"Just kidding, I don't care. C'mon, the money's around back." Without waiting, I turned and circled the house. GPS took some convincing because she hated Gordon as much as me. I tugged her a few feet before she relented. Around back there was a rotting porch and the start of the forest. The windows still had glass but the rear door was missing. I tied GPS to a tree.

"Okay, Gordon," I said.

"Okay what?"

"We need to fight it out."

"Fight?"

"Yeah." I shrugged out of my coat and hung it on a

broken branch near GPS. "I got some adrenaline going. Be fun."

"You serious?"

"I had a glove, I'd slap you with it."

Mr. Tan chuckled. "He's serious, Gibbs."

"It's the proletarian inside me. Nothing to be done."

"I'm not fighting you, asshole." He stood at the porch, gun still thrust my direction. "Tell me where the money is."

"Don't be scared, Gordon. You're the larger of us."

"Afraid of *you*? I work out for a living, shrimp."

"But I'm tougher. I hope."

"August—"

"Give the gun to Mr. Tan, Gordon. I'm going to come hit you and it'd be better if he had it. That way, it won't drop into the dirt."

"'Ey," said Mr. Tan. He indicated me with his bat. "You're carrying too. You two wanna fight it out, lose the gun."

"Whoops." I slipped the leather Bianchi holster off my belt and lovingly set the Kimber on a tree root. "Fair's fair, you're right."

"Jeez, August, why you got a gun?"

"I'm a private cop. Do the math. Wait, better not, might take til lunch."

Mr. Tan said, "Looks like a 1911."

"In fact it is. A Kimber. I grew attached to it training with the SWAT guys in Los Angeles."

"Training with SWAT?" asked Gordon. Looked like he might be shrinking.

I indicated my chin. "Put one right here, big guy."

"August, grow up."

"Get in your truck and leave, or else hit me, Gordon. Afterward, I'll tell you about the money."

"Why you want to get your ass kicked first?"

"Two reasons come to mind. First, see who wins—I'm betting on myself. Second, so you'll stop thinking you're tough."

"I work out—"

"For a living, shut up, your poor wife. I didn't say you aren't strong. But you aren't tough. Big difference," I said.

Mr. Tan held out his hand. "Gimme the gun, Gibbs. And get on with it."

"This is dumb," said Gordon.

"Gotta do it, man."

"Why?"

"Hell, I don't know. One of those things. You jumped him, now he wants to fight; you gotta," said Mr. Tan.

I agreed. "Code of honor."

He didn't want to, but Gordon pressed the gun into Mr. Tan's palm. He held the pistol easier than Gordon.

Gordon met me in the patch of dirt between the trees and the rear porch. He turned to the side and held his fists under his chin and bounced around. Hopping forwards and backwards, his shoulders rolling and exaggerated. He looked a little like a cartoon character. "Come on, bitch, let's get this done."

GPS snarled and barked.

He swung and missed, a big lumbering hook. I hit him a left in the kidney, under the ribcage; to his credit, he felt thick and sturdy and he only grunted. He threw the same big hook with the same big hand and missed again; I got him once more in the kidney, identical spot—testing him, see how tough he was. Body shots accumulate. He got close enough that he couldn't miss and took turns swinging with both fists. I caught them on my arms and shoulders. I came up with a big right, an uppercut, connected under the chin. His teeth crashed and he flailed backwards. I followed, bang

bang, jabs into his teeth. He gave ground too easy. Entirely uninterested in continuing. His heel hit the rotting porch and the momentum sat him down. Tried to get up. Tried again—he stood and swayed and righted himself. His mouth bled.

He probed the inside of his mouth with his tongue. "Shit. Think I broke a tooth."

"You're done," I said. I dropped my hands. "You already quit. Where's the resilience? Where's the grit? Does posing in front of a mirror not help with things like...reality?"

"Gimme the got'damn gun," he said. His words sounded thick. He held his hand out to Mr. Tan.

"I am morose, Gordo, that it's over so quick," I said. "Been looking forward to this for a while. I'm not even breathing hard. Colleen, the poor dissatisfied woman, this is what she must feel like."

"Gimme the gun," said Gordon again. His words produced some steam in the cold air.

"Get it? It's a joke about your ineptitude in the bedroom."

"Get in there, Gibbs. It ain't over," said Mr. Tan. "This a fight. Kick that ass."

"The gun!"

Gordon didn't say 'my' gun. It wasn't his. Clearly.

"Jeez, Gibbs. Here. Use the bat, you need to."

Gordon took it and pointed the barrel at me. "How about now, *tough* guy."

"Is this because you realized within a few seconds that you can't win?" I said. "It'd make me feel better if you verbalized it. Something about people I don't like is when they give up at the first sign of trouble."

GPS howled and pulled at her leash.

"August," said Gordon. "Last chance before I use the bat."

I said, "You're right, this way's more fair."

Manny Martinez emerged from inside the abandoned farmhouse. Dressed in casual clothes, not his marshal outfit. He took two long steps, spread his arms, and clunked the beefcakes' heads together. Skull against skull. The collision hurt and jarred them both enough that they fell. He smoothly drew his gun, lowered and pressed his knee hard into the spine of Mr. Tan, forcing him into the dirt, and Manny then inserted his gun into Mr. Tan's flared nostril.

"Aw Manny," I said. "Even with the bat, I think I woulda won."

Manny was on top of Mr. Tan. "Don't care, amigo, I was getting bored."

"Whothafugisthis," said Mr. Tan, face squished, nose plugged. Manny rightly recognized him as the greater threat. "Gedoffame, gedthegunouamyface."

Manny hit Mr. Tan with the butt of his big silver .357 Magnum and then aimed at Gordon, lying nearby. "Stay down, tubbo."

"It's *Gordo*," I said.

"Ay caramba, whatever," said Manny. Gordon tried to rise so Manny hit Mr. Tan in the head again with the butt of his gun. Opened a cut along Mr. Tan's shaved hairline. "See what happens? You get up, I hit your friend. Try and find out."

Gordon hesitated.

Manny pressed his knee harder into Mr. Tan's back.

"GibbsyoubigassholegedDOWN," groaned Mr. Tan.

"Stay down or I hit your friend again, Gordie."

"*Gordo*," I said.

"Who are—" said Gordon.

Manny aimed at Gordon and fired. A humongous noise. The blast filled our clearing to the point of pain and rebounded, startling GPS into silence. The bullet traveled not more than four inches above Gordon's head and the man cried obscenities.

"Stay down, pendejo. I might not miss again."

Gordon lowered and Manny returned the pistol to Mr. Tan's nose, and he grinned.

Two giant weightlifters cowed into stillness by a guy half their weight. But few men were as crazy as Manny—something in his voice was fearless and nasty and it connected with a nerve deep inside. The nerve told the brain, *Wait...I think this guy's almost out of control.* And he was.

I went for my gun. Clipped it onto my belt, and slipped into my jacket. I scratched GPS to reassure her. "See, Gordon. Muscle doesn't equal strength. And strength doesn't equal tough."

Manny said, "Don't think he can follow that math."

"You ruined the fun. He was going to beat me with a bat. I was going to hit him back. Real blue collar work, it would've been great."

"I'm calling the cops," said Gordon. His mouth bled onto the dirt. "Think I won't?"

Manny reached around to his belt and came back with handcuffs. He dropped them between Mr. Tan and Gordon and said, "You're in luck, señor. Cops is already here."

Gordon cursed more.

"So you—you're just gonna keep all the money, huh?" said Gordon. "Legally it belongs to Colleen."

He sat in the dead leaves at the base of a dormant maple,

his back against the trunk. Mr. Tan on the other side. Their arms were pulled backwards and hands cuffed together, circling the trunk. And there they would remain until someone freed them, their plight hopeless.

"The spouse is entitled to half of all marital assets at the time of separation," I said.

"Exactly. She should get half of the money," said Gordon.

"What money?"

He nodded at the farmhouse. "The money you're about to take. I knew that dog was worth a fortune."

"Hypothetically, if the dog led you to a fortune, would you give Ulysses half?"

He sniffed and looked away. Called me a horrible, *horrible* name.

I said, "There's no money in that house, Gordon."

"The hell there isn't. You told Colleen—"

"I tested her. Wanted to discover if she'd send you to steal it. 'Twas a mere ruse, Gordo. While she and I talked on the phone, I found this random house on a map. There's nothing inside."

Gordon set his jaw and glowered. Didn't know whether to insist there was money in the house or admit he had been tricked. Foolish either way; a sad state of affairs.

"And now I'm despondent about Colleen," I said. "I wanted her to be better."

"She just wants what she deserves, August."

"But she already got *you*, Gordo."

Manny dropped the key to their handcuffs into the dirt, beyond their reach.

I said, "I'll phone Colleen later. Alert her to your predicament and she'll come unlock you. Meantime, avoid the bears."

Manny picked up Gordon's SIG and pocketed it. He nudged the bat with his toe. "Wanna hit them a few times? Be like a piñata."

"I don't get it, August. If there's no money, why the hell did you hit me?" said Gordon Gibbs.

"Indulgence."

"Huh?"

"You tried to intimidate me since the moment we met. I bet you do that with everyone. I bet you did it with Alex Steinbeck, a girl of whom I'm fond. You're not special, Gordon. You have more mass than most, is all. I'm not special either. Well...debatable. But guys like you shouldn't lean on others with your bulk. You got a lot of fear inside and that's why you didn't want to fight me and why you demanded the gun. Afraid and mean, the sign of a bully. That's why. To show you you can't flex and run over everyone. And Gordon, I find out you're still trying to push your way through the Steinbeck family, I'm going to kick your ass again. But this time Manny won't save you. You can have the bat but I'll give you an enema with it. Understand?"

Mr. Tan made a chuckling noise. I kinda liked him. He understood honor, to a small degree, and he knew when his friend was being obtuse.

I untied Georgina Princess.

"Hey c'mon," said Gordon. He appeared close to tears. "Be serious. That dog. Is it worth a lot of money or not?"

"*Her*," I said. "And she's valuable just because she is."

32

The sun climbed higher and burned off some of the chill, and Manny and I went up Bent Mountain. At the top he parked at the old Mount Union Church and got into my rented truck. Georgina Princess jumped into the back but leaned forward enough for her head to be between ours, a situation she thought glorious.

Manny looked ashamed. "About Gordon, Mack. I'm sorry."

"You should be."

"I really wanted to clunk their heads together. I never get to do that."

"Was it great?"

"Migo, it was so great I cannot find the words."

"I shouldn't have started the fight. That was immature of me," I said.

"I enjoyed it."

"So did I. But."

"It bugged you," said Manny. "That he thought he was tougher."

"Yes."

"You know you could beat him. But you wanted him to know too."

"All of these reasons. And most of them are childish."

"No one ever claimed you're a grownup," said Manny.

"But maybe one day."

We drove halfway to Floyd and turned onto back roads, curling between undulating horizons dotted with cows. Larry Alexander owned the land. Using Google Earth, we located the ATV trail. The same trail Ulysses took with his Jeep three years ago. Same trail Alex tried to get her Audi up that fateful night.

We roared and bounced up the mountain for half an hour. A lot easier than walking through.

The burnt shed came into view and I stopped in a squeal of brakes. Manny let GPS out and she ran in circles and did jumps and rejoiced. I reached into the truck bed for a metal detector.

Manny said, "What are we doing? I forget exactly."

"Geocaching."

"Geo what?"

"Following a hunch," I said.

"I'll keep my eyes peeled for one of those."

Manny went through the Jeep for anything I missed. I used the metal detector and scraped out the wooden structure until satisfied nothing else was there, and then I walked enlarging concentric circles outward. Same as last time, the air here felt colder. Or thinner or wetter or all of it. Small animals took flight when GPS bounded near and she gave fruitless chase.

Manny spoke. His voice sounded large out here in the wild. "Think we should take up hunting?"

"Shooting deer?"

"*Simon*," he said, the Spanish equivalent for 'Yup.'

"You like venison?"

"Don't know."

"You drive a supercharged Camaro. I don't think you're allowed," I said. "The real hunters would be mean to you."

It was Georgina Princess who found it. She eagerly pawed at a spot fifteen yards out, sniffing and throwing soil. A good place, removed from the gnarliest of roots.

The metal detector screamed when I passed over.

Manny came with the shovel and said, "I know a hunch when I hear it, *hombre*."

The black earth yielded to his blade and he dug a few moments and then I took a turn. Roots had to be chopped through, and a deliberate layer of rocks plucked out piece by piece. The day was chilly but the work warm.

Twenty-four inches down, the blade connected with something firm—not a rock. We scooped with our hands to reveal a rotting blue tarp in the shape of a square. Two feet by three feet. We scooped more, aided by the tireless and valiant hound, until we found handles on the side.

We each took a handle and dead-lifted the thing out from the compact soil. It was a heavy-duty storage chest. Water proof. Sealed tight and wrapped with a tarp for good measure. I pulled the tarp and the fibers parted. Manny hacked at the lock with his shovel. The lock didn't break but the housing did, rusted through by long exposure to soil and water.

I knelt. Ripped the lock and housing off. Pushed at the lid but it didn't budge. Manny inserted the shovel blade under the lid and pushed down, prying it open. I threw the lid back and we looked inside.

"Ay dios mio," said Manny.

"Right? I'm so good at this it's scary."

———————

33

The next day, Rose Bridges brought Ulysses Steinbeck to my office. Until now I'd only seen him within his home and I realized I thought of him as an invalid, a man incapable of leaving his house. But he strode into my office and looked as a handsome radiologist should.

Georgina Princess waited in the corner, smiling. I'd asked her to stay there and she obeyed. Like a princess.

I shook his hand and said, "Dr. Steinbeck, I'm Mackenzie August. Thanks for coming."

He smiled politely. Maybe a flicker of recognition. "Mr. August. I'm eager to hear what you found."

"You remember?"

He patted the leather satchel slung from his shoulder. "I read up on the way over. I know enough and I'll keep reviewing the notes throughout our meeting. You smell familiar, so that helps."

"I smell as a man ought."

"That's the dog?" asked Steinbeck, sitting in one of four chairs I'd placed in the middle of my room. "I hoped seeing it would jog something loose, but...there's nothing."

Rose smiled shyly and said, "May I pet her?"

"She would like that above all things."

Rose got on her knees near GPS and scratched and spoke softly, and the dog whined and tried to lick her face.

"You remember her."

"Of course," said Rose. She stood and wiped her eyes and I held out a newly purchased box of tissues. "I took care of her for several weeks. She's still beautiful."

Dr. Steinbeck watched without emotion. "Remind me the animal's name?"

"Georgina Princess Steinbeck."

He took out a journal and pen and scratched.

Four chairs in the middle of the room—my swivel chair brought from around the desk, my two client chairs, and I borrowed a straight-back from the commercial realtor down the hall. In the middle, I had arranged a carafe of coffee steaming beside three mugs.

I said, "Is Roanoke constantly fresh and new in your eyes?"

Dr. Steinbeck grunted. Almost a smile—mostly grim but with some humor. "There used to be a restaurant below us. Metro. Rose tells me this is the third time I've asked about its closure."

"Closed two years ago, I think."

"After my accident." He sighed and aimed it upward. "So in my mind, it'll be there forever."

We made small talk for five minutes and Alex Steinbeck walked in. She wore leather boots with no heel and black leggings with a wide leather belt that had no function and a black vest (trying to look like Han Solo?). She entered warily and with her guard up but the defense melted at the sight of her father. I hadn't told each about the other. She lit up and dazzled, worth a hundred thousand likes or favorites or hearts or whatever social media button it was. Ulysses grabbed her and they hugged and both cried a little. Only an hour's drive separated them but reunions like this must not happen enough.

She hugged Rose too, and the elder of the two looked relieved.

"Oh this has to be Georgina Princess," said Alex and she scratched the dog all over. "What a good girl. What a beautiful and perfect girl. You have me nervous, Mr. August. Why're we all here?"

"It's good news." I indicated the chairs situated around the coffee and mugs, which rested charmingly on a table-cloth-covered box. "Help yourself."

We all sat. GPS laid beside my chair.

"I'm too scared for coffee," said Alex.

"And I'm ready for answers," said Ulysses.

Alex smiled a sad but content smile as she watched her father write in the journal.

"Should I be here?" asked Rose. "I can wait in the car."

"You belong, Rose. Trust me."

A half grimace from her. Everyone was anxious.

"I think I've uncovered a lot of truth and history, and it's good news for everyone in this room, and it'll be better if we all hear it together. Ready?"

No one answered.

Mackenzie August, riveting entertainment.

Here we go.

"Ulysses Steinbeck wakes up every day having forgotten what happened yesterday, and the day before that, all the way back to some hazy time months before the accident. He cannot concretely remember details from this time of haze before the accident, but his mind knows he's neglected *something* important. Something he meant to do but the crash prevented it, and it has something to do with the dog."

All three nodded. Ulysses appeared relieved that all this matched up with his notes and his tenuous understanding of the situation.

I proceeded. "So he hires me to find the dog and I do, but it leads to more and more questions, and soon my mission is no longer to simply find the dog but to instead find out *why* he wants the dog. And I have. It'll make more sense if I recreate the events leading up to the crash three years ago."

Alex changed her mind about the coffee. She leaned forward and poured a mug and took it from the box between us.

"Four years ago, approximately, Colleen and Ulysses are drifting apart. There's no animosity or rage or screaming, there's simply distance and apathy. This is a natural occurrence without hard work on the part of both partners. Even though both Colleen and Ulysses want the divorce, it does not come without consequences. Primarily for Alex, it's devastating. But also for Colleen and Ulysses. I haven't researched her much, but I can tell that Ulysses was flailing. He had all the hallmarks of a man in crisis. It probably didn't help that Colleen was having an affair with Gordon Gibbs, professional muscle man."

He stopped writing on the page. He closed his eyes and took steadying breaths. Alex placed her hand on his arm and squeezed.

"Even though the divorce was amiable and consensual, it hurt. And Ulysses hated Gordon. So before the marital assets could be divided, Ulysses emptied their savings account and flew to Monaco and gambled. This was the first in a bizarre series of events out of character for Ulysses, but the march of time and accumulating pain and desperation have ways of changing us, and he was a changed man. Wildly so."

Rose and Alex both nodded. Ulysses listened intently, too interested to document.

I said, "Somewhere during this time of upheaval, Ulysses and Rose became romantic. I suspect it was after the gambling trip."

Rose went white. Dr. Steinbeck cleared his throat and Alex held her breath.

Rose whispered, "You know?"

"I know. Dr. Steinbeck, there's something you need to understand—Rose is one of my favorite people on earth. The evidence has mounted during my investigation, allowing me to determine that Rose is a saint and you're beyond lucky to have her.

Some of the color returned to Rose's cheeks and her eyes teared. Ulysses looked both shy and alarmed, like his dirty little secret was out.

"Alex," I continued. "There's something you need to understand, too—your father proposed to Rose before the accident."

Alex's posture became more erect. She said, "You're kidding."

"I am not. I guessed you didn't know."

"No, I... Dad, is that true?"

"I..." He blinked and fumbled absently at his journals. "I-I'm not sure. It's..."

I held up my hand. "Let me answer the question. It's not fair for Ulysses or Rose either to try. Yes, he proposed. There's photographic evidence but Rose doesn't show it off. Ulysses can't remember it, which means he wakes up each day with a huge crush on Rose but unsure if it's safe to admit it. And Rose, bless her perfect heart, can never tell anyone about the secret engagement. If they got married now, Ulysses wouldn't remember. And she knows the union would be one of scorn and derision because the public doesn't know the truth and wouldn't be convinced anyway. They'd think the caretaker just wanted more money. Here's a guess—Alex, you found out about the secret romance the night of the crash. And another guess—you were furious. The divorce crushed you, and then you find him with the housekeeper and then the car accident...I bet you blamed her for a while. Even though it wasn't her fault. There's no way she could tell you the truth. So instead Rose stays with the man she loves and works in silence, and I think she's a hero on par with Mother Teresa."

Rose had been crying quietly but now she issued a loud sob. I handed her the box of freshly purchased tissues and she took several and cried into them.

Alex leaned into Rose and put her arms around her. My opinion of Alex was almost as high as that of Rose. Alex said, "Rose! You could have told me, I would believe you. Oh my gosh, Rose..."

Ulysses set his journals down and got on his knees at the feet of the two girls and he put his arms around both and they wept as one.

I let them talk and hug for several minutes. I debated taking a photograph with my phone and using it for marketing purposes. Mackenzie August—he'll make you cry but it's for your own good; just look at this beautiful family he fixed.

GPS observed the emotional outburst with concern until I placed my hand on her neck.

Eventually order was restored. Ulysses moved into the chair next to Rose and held her hand. Rose dabbed at her eyes with a tissue and said, "Thank you, Mr. August. But I don't believe it does much good. Ulysses will forget soon."

"It matters, Rose."

"He's right," said Alex. "It *matters*. It matters that I know. All this time I thought Dad had been having a fling."

"And—" I said.

"And you two should get married!" said Alex with enough enthusiasm and energy to power a city block. "Why wouldn't you?"

"Because he won't remember."

"So *what?* He can discover it each day. I'm making this happen, Rose. On a beach somewhere. Just our closest friends. I want you as a member of the family. Officially."

"Absolutely," said Ulysses. "Every time I remember it'll bring fresh joy."

Rose, bless her heart, cried more.

Ulysses continued, "You should be a Steinbeck. If I had a ring, I'd propose on my knees right now."

Rose took a steadying breath. "You two are sweet. And you make me very happy. But I couldn't manage it."

"Don't worry; I'll handle everything. This Spring when it's warm. You will just show up beautiful. That's your whole responsibility" said Alex. In that moment, I would've taken a bullet for her. Or at least, thrown Manny in front of the bullet.

Ulysses resumed scribbling. He didn't want to forget this.

I said, "Rose, I'm curious. When did you and Ulysses become romantic?"

"I fell in love with him a long time ago, but never told anyone. Least of all him. Soon after he discovered his wife with Gordon Gibbs, he fell into depression. And my heart broke for him. We started talking more. He would stay at home days when he knew I was coming. Bought me flowers. The tension between us grew, but still...it wasn't until he returned from Monaco that...as you say, he was changed. The romance began then."

"Mr. August, what does this have to do with Georgina Princess?" said Alex.

"Good question. Let's continue the story. So Ulysses and Colleen file for divorce. Something like that wrecks us. We feel like we're failures, and based on the evidence he felt it acutely. Ulysses was in free fall. And my guess is, suddenly he wanted to become a better father."

Rose nodded and looked at her sudden fiancé. "He did."

Alex snapped her fingers. "I remember that! I started getting a lot more attention. He came to my games and bought me presents."

"Including...?"

"Including Georgina Princess."

"That's right. You'd always wanted a dog but couldn't have one. Now your dad will get you anything you want," I said. "So he surprises you with a puppy. But not just any puppy. That's not enough."

"Not just any puppy? What do you mean?"

I reached down to pat Georgina Princess around the ribs. She sighed with pleasure. "If you inspect the dog's skin, through here, you'll find markings."

"What kind?" asked Alex.

"A tattoo. GPS coordinates."

Ulysses's pen stopped. He squinted and said, "Huh. That's...how about that. I remember it. Kind of."

Rose frowned. "I don't understand. Who would tattoo a dog with GPS coordinates?"

"A man on fire. A man who didn't particularly care how dogs felt about being tattooed."

Alex whacked her father with the back of her hand. "Dad! You tattooed a *puppy?*"

"Maybe. I don't...it rings a bell."

"That's why she had the bandage when you brought her home," said Alex, eyes round and horrified. "It wasn't a wound, it was a tattoo. What were you thinking?"

"I have no idea."

"I do," I said. "Who can guess where the coordinates lead to?"

"I'm stumped," said Alex. "This is wild."

"I have a guess," said Rose, shyly. "To the shed in the woods?"

"Bingo." I shot her with my finger.

"That's why Ulysses knew the GPS coordinates, the night he burned himself. I thought that was odd," said Rose. She looked a little strained with the painful memory.

"Why...I'm confused," said Alex. "Why tattoo a dog with the location of that shack in the woods?"

"Remember, the dog was intended for you," I said.

"So?"

"So the tattoo was for you also."

"As in, that old shack is mine?" she said.

"No. It belongs to a nice man named Larry Alexander. Rose, let me guess about this part. One day, Ulysses says he wants to show you a secret. So he takes you in his Jeep to the woods. Way out in the middle of nowhere to an old wooden shack. He has a secret to share with you, he says. He also brings wine and candles. Right?"

She nods. "That's exactly right."

"He doesn't drink, but he's a changed man. It's just you and him and it's kinda romantic and he starts drinking and keeps going and he lights candles and soon he's sick and accidentally sets the shack on fire."

She nodded more. Twisting the tissue in her fingers.

Ulysses, writing furiously, says, "Doesn't sound like me."

"Rose is drunk in the middle of the woods, and Ulysses is drunk and badly injured. Rose doesn't want to call the police or an ambulance because Colleen would find out they're together and it might make things tricky. The divorce isn't finalized yet. So they call Alex. And we all know what happened that night."

No one spoke.

I love a good audience.

"Here's what *should* have happened. Ulysses and Rose have a pleasant evening. Wine and candles, it's lovely. He shares the secret. They come home. Divorce is finalized. They get married. Alex gets the puppy. And sometime later, Ulysses decides it's time to share the secret with his daughter."

"*What* secret?" said Alex.

"He tattooed the dog because that shack is a hard place to find, and the puppy would be a more meaningful and grand gesture that way. Or at least, to a mind on fire. Plus, Ulysses couldn't safely give you the gift until later, when you were older."

"What gift? Please Mr. August, this is torture."

I stood and picked up the carafe and mugs and set them aside. I tugged aside the tablecloth to reveal the box underneath. A waterproof storage container with the lock ripped off.

I said, "This was buried at the shack. It's for you, Alex."

"For me?"

"The tattoo on the dog led to these coordinates. It's yours. Open it."

She did, with trembling fingers. The lid pushed back and she gasped. So did Rose.

The box was stuffed with various currencies. Stacks and stacks of hundred dollar bills, secured with rubber bands. Stacks of euros in denominations of 100 and 500. Trays full of poker chips from casinos in Monaco and Las Vegas, thousands worth. Silver and gold coins too.

"What...I don't..." she said, fingers trembling.

"Read the note," I said.

On top was an envelope. She opened it, pulled out a letter, and read.

My dearest Alex,

*I hope one day you'll forgive me for my hasty trip to Europe. With the looming divorce, Colleen's boyfriend will soon be entitled to half of my assets. Half of **your** assets, Alexandra. And I cannot abide that. I didn't work this hard for some dense slab of hamburger to open up more gyms with my money.*

So here it is.

It is yours, approximately two million dollars.

Spend it wisely and slowly, so Gordon Gibbs will never catch on. If he's still alive—I suspect a steroidal aneurysm any day will stop his brain. Or should I say, I hope for one.

Don't worry about me. I'll make more.

Your loving father.

The note passed back and forth between them. Even Ulysses was stunned.

I said, "Ulysses didn't go to Monaco to gamble. He went to launder cash. A casino is a great place to do that. Over the course of several days, he slowly bought more and more chips. He cashed some out for euros. He went to Las Vegas and did the same thing there. He kept some of the money in poker chips to avoid suspicion at the cashier. If Colleen pressed the issue, he had receipts for large sums. Gambling losses are hard to verify."

Ulysses scratched at his mane of thick hair. "I—I must really have been out of sorts. I cannot imagine going through with such a scheme."

"You panicked. You were broken and hurting and lost. And you hated Gordon. Which," I said. "Is understandable."

Alex's fingers burrowed into the coins. She looked at the open container with amazement and some fear. "So...what now?"

"That's up for you to decide. My job is finished."

"But, please? Mr. August, I don't know what to do."

"Here are some thoughts, if you insist. Pay for your college degree. Pay for counseling sessions. Fund a retirement account for your father and Rose. And for yourself. Maybe pay for the wedding. Go on a nice trip."

"But...I think Rose and Dad should take it back."

"That works too," I said. "This is a judgment free zone, and I don't blame anyone for wanting to bilk Gordon Gibbs —but keep in mind half of it legally belongs to Colleen."

"I want her to have some, too," said Alex. She stared at the container without seeing it. "Maybe set up a retirement account for her also? I don't know if she has much money now."

"Up to you. If you need advice, seek it from Rose. She might be the most selfless woman I know."

Rose looked as though one more surprise today might kill her.

"We have only one final item to discuss. And she's the most important on the docket." I reached down to scratch Georgina Princess behind the ears.

34

Case closed.

Ulysses was satisfied, Alex wasn't broke, and Rose was over the moon with joy. And I? I went home for lunch, feeling smug about a job well done.

Ol' Mack August, worth every penny.

I pushed open the front door and Georgina Princess August bolted inside first. She ran circles throughout the main floor and went up and down the stairs a few times.

My favorite girl was cooking in the kitchen, the loveliest of all sights.

Ronnie said, "How'd it go?"

"I'm worth every penny."

"You're worth every million, Mackenzie." She wore no shoes and she moved around on the balls of her feet, something she did without thinking, like a dancer. She wore straight-legged Paige khakis and a red apron...and that was it. Nothing else under the red apron. "What will you do now?"

"Not sure. Might go kill Darren Robbins."

"I approve. I'll pay you for your time."

"Your outfit is to die for," I told her, coming to rest on a kitchen stool.

She leaned far enough over the counter to kiss me. "Everyone is at work, and Kix is at Roxanne's, so…"

"So you cook naked?"

"I'm not naked. I have on pants. I'm making Italian sausage and vegetable soup."

"What if something spatters?" I said.

"The apron covers what it needs to. Mostly. Isn't this charming? It's like I'm your doting wife from the 50's."

"Honey, I'm home."

"Does Georgina Princess belong to the August household now?"

"She does," I said.

"Perfect. I'd grown fond of her." She turned to the stove to stir the pot and I admired her shoulders and the arch of her spine."

"Did you have court this morning?"

"I did. Judge Rowe. He adores me."

"Why wouldn't he."

"I got you something," she said and she slid a plate my way. The plate was covered with shredded paper. "A gift."

"Thanks, I was hoping for some confetti."

"It's an apology."

"I can tell," I said shrewdly.

"An apology for being a mess. I was making this difficult. Making *us* difficult, I mean. My psychosis and insecurities were wrecking things."

"Oh?"

"Don't Oh? me. You knew it already. But I'm still learning."

"What are you learning?" I asked.

"You love me. Even if you've never said the words, you do."

"I do."

"It's that simple. You treat me like you love me, and you're not going to stop. Loving someone shouldn't be complex. That's hard for me to process. You're committed to me and that doesn't make sense, and I have to force myself to realize it several times a day. I'm still new, and I was trying to make us something else. But...I'm watching you and I'm learning, and I think it's simple. If you love someone, you love them. It's a verb."

"Yes."

She stirred the pot absently. "This will be tricky. Because I think I love me more than I love you."

"You summed up the central pillar of human frailty and brokenness with that revelation."

"It's a breath-taking revelation. To realize that I'm even more broken than I thought."

"And," I said. "To realize I'm more broken than you thought."

"Yes. That's why the wedding ceremony matters to you. Or at least the exchange of vows. It's a promise to *do*. And you want to say those promises out loud, so we can hear each other and the world can hear them. Because that's what you take the most seriously. Promises to act and live a certain way. And if I had half a brain in my head, I'd realize how important it is for me too."

"Well articulated."

"Okay. So...moment of truth." She closed her eyes and took a deep breath, a motion I admired. "And I want you to be honest. Need you to. I know you love me. You don't even need to say it, because every act of your life states it. You love me. But...do you want to be locked into that? Because that's what a wedding ceremony is. You're already doing it, but after a wedding you're not allowed to stop. Because you're a man who keeps his promises."

"Are you the kind of girl who keeps hers?"

"You know I'm not. Or at least, I never have been. But you also know that I'm trying to become good. It's not really fair for you to be tethered to someone who isn't...there yet. So, do you truly want a wedding ceremony and vows? If you want to wait, I'm not going to leave. I know you wouldn't leave me. And besides, I'm head over heels for you."

"You realize you're swinging the jury by only wearing an apron."

"Of course. I'll do anything to influence your vote in my favor. But, Mackenzie, if you want the wedding ceremony then let's not make a big thing out of it. I'm not a girl who wants a guy to get on his knees and propose. I don't want to send out announcements or have people take pictures while we shove cake at each other. I don't even need a ring."

"No ring?"

"I don't need one. And to show you how committed I am, look at your gift again." She indicated the plate with shredded paper. "That's our annulment. I filled it out last week, because I thought you wanted it. But I changed my mind and shredded it. I'm not giving you an annulment. I want you. Forever."

I felt warm from my toes to my nose. "Wow."

"You want an annulment, go through another attorney. And I'll fight it."

I grinned. She smiled back. The air between us thrummed. "You're talking a lot, Ronnie."

"I'm nervous, Mackenzie. I just told a beautiful man that I love him but I would understand if he can't commit to me yet. It's harrowing."

"I have a suggestion," I said.

"I'm all ears."

"Not at the moment you're not. I can't seem to get my eyes above your collarbone."

"I'll rephrase. I'm all yours, Mackenzie. What's the suggestion?"

"You may not want a ring, but..." I reached into my pocket and pulled out a small velvet box. Opened it and placed it on the counter. "Here's one anyway. Let's be engaged."

She dropped the wooden spoon onto the floor. Inhaled strongly enough for me to hear oxygen flood her lungs. Her hand went to her throat, and her chest and neck and cheeks flushed.

She whispered, "But we're already married."

"Let's be both."

"I was wrong. I was so wrong about the ring." She picked it up and a big perfect tear filled and went over her cheekbone and disappeared under her jaw. "I love this one so much. I'm keeping it."

"Forever."

She came around the table and rested against me, half in my lap. She slid the ring onto her finger—perfect; I'd measured with another she wore occasionally. "It's perfect. And gigantic."

"Two carats. I used my savings. You might need to pay for dinner the next month."

"Mackenzie."

"Yes Ronnie."

"One day soon, we'll exchange vows. I want to make promises to you. Promises I'll keep." She pressed her face into my neck and sighed. "You're my husband *and* my fiancé.

And we have a dog, and I'm more content and happy than I thought possible."

"Me too. And we haven't even tried the soup yet."

"Mackenzie. I've been topless under this apron for thirty minutes, and I've been thinking about you the whole time, and you just gave me an engagement ring, and I'm all kinds of aroused."

"Now you know how I feel incessantly. Should we go upstairs?"

Her fingers played with my collar. "Or on the couch or wherever. I want my fiancé to take off this apron immediately."

"But my wife might get jealous."

"You can have us both, Mackenzie. For always."

EPILOGUE

Fat Susie drove Veronica Summers to Washington D.C. on a crisp Tuesday morning, ten days after her unexpected engagement. She rode in the back seat diligently working and accumulating billable hours.

Outside the federal courthouse in Alexandria, she met up with her client, Mateo Hernández, and Fat Susie remained in the car. Mateo had been waiting three months for this hearing, only a week before his deportation.

Inside, they waited their turn in court and Ms. Summers successfully argued on Mateo's behalf for an adjustment of status, and an hour later they emerged again into the sun; Mateo the proud owner of a green card.

It helped that Mateo had money.

It helped that Judge Reeves frequently daydreamed about his counselor.

Veronica got back into the Mercedes, a thick envelope of cash hidden inside her Saint Laurent crocodile handbag— the Hernández family left no paper trails.

"Where to?" said Fat Susie, watching her in the rearview. "Home?"

"I need coffee first, please, Reginald. I like The Spot. Jamieson."

"Can do."

Fat Susie parked a block from The Spot and they walked. It was mid-morning and the coffee shop was empty, the early commuters already at work. She ordered coffee for both and sat at a booth with her phone. Fat Susie went to the restroom.

Had she been more vigilant, she would have noticed two men enter The Spot, and the barista leave out the back. She would have noticed the large man walk to the restroom and lock the door with a key. No one getting in or out.

She looked up, startled, as Darren Robbins slid into the booth across from her.

"Oh shit," she said. "And my day was going so well."

"Good to see you too, doll."

She rolled her eyes, fighting down a quiver of fear in her chest. "Really, Darren? We're going to play this game here?"

Darren Robbins was dressed in an overcoat and black gloves. He had short wavy brown hair. A handsome guy, though everyone thought his eyes were an unsettling shade of brown and green. "An engagement ring. Congratulations, Ron. Based on the tiny stone, I assume you're marrying a broke cop."

"I'm through with boys, Darren," she said and she flicked her gaze over him. A mocking smile. "Tell all your boyfriends, the limp old men you coddle. I'm taken."

"You think that rookie can protect you? Or himself?"

"You already tried to kill him. The entire underworld gathered in Naples and it wasn't enough. Mackenzie is a man you can't even hope to become."

He grabbed her hand. So quick she couldn't react, so

firm she couldn't pull free. He pinched her fingers and it hurt.

"Where's he now?" he said. "At home. On the sidelines."

"Let go, Darren," she said through clenched teeth. "You don't own me anymore."

"Yeah. I heard."

Only now did she realize The Spot had emptied. Foolish to come here, especially considering who owned it. The only other person in The Spot was a man standing at the door. She'd never seen a man so large. He was of Hispanic descent, probably close to seven-feet tall and impossibly thick and broad. His tattooed arms were crossed. Had wore no expression.

The hairs on Ronnie's arms raised.

"I got an idea, Ron," said Darren. "I cut a deal with you and the broke cop in Roanoke. Gets me out of your hair forever."

"Sounds too good to be true," she replied.

The giant came to their table, towering over both. Trapping Ronnie.

Behind her, a bang at the men's bathroom door. Fat Susie, locked in and no help.

Darren smiled, a sight that made Veronica sick. "I didn't say you were gonna like it."

A note from the author -

I HOPE you enjoyed *Good Girl*. A lighter book was in order after *Aces Full* and *Only the Details*.

YOU PROBABLY HATED THE EPILOGUE. My apologies.

BUT GOOD NEWS! The next book is ready for you to read. Mackenzie's latest client is Darren Robbins, and he's got a case Mackenzie can't afford to lose.

"The other books in the series are good, but this one is the best." - Amazon Review of *These Mortals*, book seven.

IT MAY INTEREST you to know Alan Lee is a pen name—my real name is Alan Janney.

I wrote a series of young adult books under Alan Janney, and I didn't want a pack of thirteen-year-olds reading the Mackenzie series, and that's why I write under Alan Lee (my middle name).

IF YOU'D LIKE to follow me on Instagram, find me at Author-AlanJanney.

I WROTE a short story about the honeymoon of Ronnie and Mackenzie in the Bahamas. It takes place after *Only the Details* and before *Good Girl*, and involves a minor mystery, and it didn't fit in either book. So if you'd like to read it, **click here and I'll email it to you for free. The short story is called A Ghost in Paradise.**

FINAL THING! If you haven't tried the series about Manny, it is time. Trust me. They are thrillers, not mysteries, but you'll like them. If you don't trust me, trust the reviews. Click here. It's for your own good.